I FEAR MY PAIN
INTERESTS YOU

I FEAR MY PAIN INTERESTS YOU

A novel

by
Stephanie LaCava

VERSO
London • New York

First published by Verso 2022
© Stephanie LaCava 2022

1 3 5 7 9 10 8 6 4 2

Verso
UK: 6 Meard Street, London W1F 0EG
US: 388 Atlantic Avenue, Suite 1010, Brooklyn, NY 11217
versobooks.com

Verso is the imprint of New Left Books

ISBN-13: 978-1-83976-602-2
ISBN-13: 978-1-83976-603-9 (UK EBK)
ISBN-13: 978-1-83976-604-6 (US EBK)

British Library Cataloguing in Publication Data
A catalogue record for this book is available from the British Library

Library of Congress Cataloging-in-Publication Data

Names: LaCava, Stephanie, author.
Title: I fear my pain interests you : a novel / by Stephanie LaCava.
Description: First edition paperback. | London ; New York : Verso, 2022.
Identifiers: LCCN 2022003526 (print) | LCCN 2022003527 (ebook) | ISBN
  9781839766022 (paperback) | ISBN 9781839766039 (UK ebk) | ISBN
  9781839766046 (US ebk)
Subjects: LCGFT: Novels.
Classification: LCC PS3612.A29 I34 2022 (print) | LCC PS3612.A29 (ebook)
  | DDC 813/.6—dc23/eng/20220127
LC record available at https://lccn.loc.gov/2022003526
LC ebook record available at https://lccn.loc.gov/2022003527

Typeset in Electra by Biblichor Ltd, Edinburgh
Printed and bound by CPI Group (UK) Ltd, Croydon CR0 4YY

To E. K.

Cows are not sentient beings

—Reddit

I Fear
My Pain
Interests You

A NOVEL

Stephanie LaCava

I

The mirror in the plane bathroom had fingerprints all over it and fog-thick grease where the soap had back-splashed. One hour into the flight, plenty of hands had been busy here. I scooted in and pushed at the latch with a knuckle. The light flickered and brightened but the bolt stuck midway. I swallowed hard and drew a paper towel to wipe the glass. The grease was still there, I'd just spread it around. I pushed down the faucet and destroyed the soft-bodied soap-thing, then ran my finger under the drip and tried the stain again, not its reflection on my skin. And the mirror cleared, to show flesh and marks of teeth.

I looked away and pulled two more towels from the dispenser and put them down on the toilet seat. The sheet on the left sucked itself to the plastic ring, catching urine, shrinking. The broken light flashed like a strobe. Bright, then half-dark. I pulled down my jeans and lowered myself slowly, trying not to touch anything. There was a sudden burst of turbulence and I dropped onto the seat, turning my head to see my face.

I saw the indentation below my bottom lip where I had been biting down. Lit by the blue pallor of the light above, the red streak appeared half-black, like in an old movie or cartoon, or an X-ray machine, like the skeleton of electrocution through a shocked body. Another brand in black and blue. This had happened before, broken skin begetting scars. Like when I gnawed my thumbnail and made the quick bleed. I would taste it, touch my face. My eyelids drooped and I sat there, head in hands.

Five times people tried to enter and five times I ignored them. Fist rapping, dramatic sigh, exasperated breaths coming closer as the person eyeballs the "CANT" on the lock.

"Someone's been in there a really long time," my latest persecutor said loudly. Turbulence hit again and I bit on that poor piece of face again as my head jerked down, brushing against the hinge in the door. The light flickered and I looked up. The gold of my choker lit a spark in the mirror. My left hand still held my chin. My right flew to my forehead covering my eyes. My ass—still dry on the right-hand side, at least—clenched spasmodically. I stayed that way until a sixth person banged on the door. It could have been hours, but the flight only lasted two and I'd watched half an action film already. A silent action film. I refused the headphones.

"One minute."

I stood up and buttoned my jeans, turned around and angled my foot to press down the lever. There was the blue light-up dot high on the facing grey wall. Then, the overhead light again, illuminating a dust cloud in the stale air.

I kicked backward into where the door flexed. It gave, and I slid out, barely enough space to get past the waiting man. I had to stop myself from kneeing him reflexively. My body felt tangled, stoppered-up, violent.

How much longer until we landed in Bozeman? Would I be allowed to wander up and down the aisles until then? Make a scene. "Her face was bleeding, and she wouldn't sit back down." Only white beyond the porthole windows. I decided to regain my seat and study the foldout cartoons on how to escape in an emergency.

In the air somewhere above Montana, because of the Director's betrayal. And the comfort of him not knowing where in the world I'd landed, of him not seeing me again until there I was, writ large on some poster or movie screen. The hum of thinking this numbed the reality. It was how my mother still had to face my father after she'd left. Not across the table, but in the Paris metro. His face magnified on a poster on a platform wall. Look at my face. Does this make you remember me? A blank of the reality.

I knew the Director had the strange ability to put blinders inside his head cavity. Like a baby when his mother ducks behind the couch for the plastic ball. He's all alone. She has gone from his world! The Director communicated with you in the early stages of a play like you weren't there to begin with. Every message to the future read as blank. You can answer if you want, no obligation. Some cut and paste. A conversation with himself; any response would be beside the point. He didn't evolve, *you* adapted. He never checked his phone when he wanted it that way. When he wanted to be elsewhere, a call soon came.

3

A run-in is always a possibility when work is a common project. And this would run in and out, off and on. My work meant showing up in a local theater or playhouse or on smaller screens. I could try to be in his hands again, making choices, gaming auditions and agents, climbing and webbing. Running around pretending, mastering my thoughts and body. My parents had tried to escape each other at "work," except they were forever united by it. Professionalism leaks out all around. "All Around" was the name of one of my mother's near-hits.

Lucy was right. She said to beware of casting myself as a victim. I may have wanted something else, but I stayed for what wasn't offered. It wasn't abuse. Not this time, anyway.

I waited in the aisle by my row for a few seconds until the woman with the purple-rim plastic visor looked up through her pane of cheap iridescence. She turned back to the tiny screen of the facing seat, pulling her knees up over her belly. I let my back obstruct her view of the movie for an extra spiteful second. She inhaled, annoyed. I bit my lip harder as I closed my eyes and sat down. Turning my face away from her, I pressed into the oval porthole. I used to do this as a child on the train. Close your eyes, push your head into a corner. The colors will come. I pulled down the plastic blind and tried to wedge my head into the shallow corner.

A memory of being in a train car. I touched my chin and it was wet. The back of my hand swiped it clean. A grid of coordinates from the stain in the bathroom mirror registering my body's orientation. Dried red on my sleeve from an earlier swipe. How much longer? The intercom answered. The local temperature at Bozeman Yellowstone International Airport. Seatbelt. I kicked my backpack farther under the seat in front. The woman next to me had shifted from annoyance to disgust. She stared at my chin through her face shield. I looked away and closed my eyes again so I wouldn't have to meet hers. She started tapping my clean hand on the armrest between us. I breathed in hard, trying to calm myself. Look at her. That unnecessary face shield, an artifact from a recent past that already felt an age ago. The early style, before they grew more ergonomic, thinner. "Lady, your chin," she said. "Or maybe your nose is bleeding?"

I found a clean bit of sleeve on my forearm and held it up against my face, as bandage and wall. She looked away, edged closer to the aisle. Now I tried to meet her eyes. She was afraid of me. And we both had to stay there until landing.

Last time I'd flown it had been the opposite, I was an attraction for my seatmate. He had identified me by the mark at my hairline. "Hi, I'm Jay. I'm a fan of your mother's." Her kind of acolytes were like this, devoted. They knew about all the little things. Like my birthmark. Every one of them had a memory of a gig or a song. They always had something they wanted to tell me.

The worst ones wanted to talk about the couple, Rose Reeder and Steve Highsmith. About how she was from a music family and he was from . . . outside Detroit. About how they had The House, and all these sincere ideals and dread of selling out. About collectives and self-parody. About dropping in and dropping out. About Rose leaving

Steve to go off with the other guy in an attempt to disappear. Did they not get that these were my parents; that I was the only person alive to have already, and exhaustively, thought through all these things? Like my father's face looming in the metro, these strangers' secondhand hot takes changed people into outsize reproductions.

Unlike Jay, the lady with the face shield cared only to prevent me bleeding or sneezing anywhere near her. Near her in the sky. Like at the end of a relationship, sensing that someone itches to get away but feels they have to stay a little longer. She kept her body jammed to the aisle side. I kept my head pressed to the wall. Up close, I could see the surface was printed with faint violet spirals. The wheels dropped and the plane landed. I straightened up, the woman flipped her hair and said, "Lady, you should deal with that." I pulled the collar of my t-shirt over my nose like a mask. She seemed satisfied by this gesture and stood up, turning to the overhead compartment. The color of the arms of her shield matched that of her rolling luggage. I waited until everyone left, stood up, and put my backpack on.

I walked out of the plane, round the accordion bend of the bridge, like the top part of the plastic straws I remember from the coffee shop as a child. Lucy had told me the airport was small, but it was smaller and warmer than I expected. There were yellow wooden beams and bronze effigies of wildlife. The carpet was a crosshatch of eggplant and green. The one souvenir shop sold stuffed moose and bears, M&Ms, and tabloids with neon headlines:

"Rachel's Turning 15! I Don't Want to be Famous Like My Mom."

"Jennifer & Will Burying the Hatchet after 20 Years!"

"Reboots and Revivals Coming Soon!"

A few paces and I was past check-in on the way out. There were women and men in purple navy polyester vests. The plaster walls were camouflaged in gray-beige marbling. After two vitrines of dinosaur remains, I exited onto the Montana street.

I realized I hadn't brought a coat or anything warm enough, really. The autopilot rush of getting here from New York had been the most I could handle. I touched my neck, flicked the gold trim of the choker, then felt for the plastic clips on the base sides of my backpack; buckles where you could tighten the straps. I grasped one in each hand and steered myself forward.

There was an older woman waiting on the sidewalk, making expectant eye contact, holding a heart-shaped mylar balloon. It had been a long time since I'd been somewhere that smelled like this. Whiffs of pine and weed and gasoline. I noticed the woman with the visor standing at the curb, signaling to a black sedan. She looked back at me and then away, as if she didn't want me to know I still figured in her cares. She crossed the street towards the breezeway.

I wanted to call a cab, but I had forgotten Lucy's address. It was way back deep in our text messages, messages in which we'd gone over and over what had happened with the Director until none of it made any sense, where she said what needed to be said again and again. That he was an asshole. That I was not a victim. And this line from Chantal Akerman she often quoted: "*Souvent je ressasse et je travaille autour du manque, du rien, comme dit encore ma mère."*

All her references came from her father, the late critic Christopher James. He was born in Oregon but ended up in Paris in the late '60s. When Lucy was born, he was fifty-seven and had just wrapped his one and only movie, bankrolled by Godard. He then retired to the small town outside of Livingston, Montana where right now I was planning to stay indefinitely. He and Lucy's mom, Patricia, had a place with a studio out back where he would write and watch movies. I scrolled to the photo Lucy had sent me of the house with the address: 57 Plinth Road. Copy and paste. In three minutes, a minivan was on the way to pick me up.

I refreshed my email and saw that my father had sent the contact details of ten music friends. There was a band called Silkworm who came from nearby, and the widow of the drummer lived close to Bozeman. His list contained people who were "decent, Margot." Always repeating my name. "They will help you hide away, because they are always trying to hide themselves." My father added that I should consider taking this time to pause the acting, to write my own stuff, to look for local theater productions, something more *real*. Arriving in Montana would not be unlike arriving on set. New location, unfamiliar crew. Here we go, the same story heard over and over again, but in reverse. A Hollywood-type thing: girl leaves small town for the big city. Shared stories and lyrics. From one bad relationship to the next. Fled to the Pacific Northwest. I thought I could get away from songwriters and filmmakers and the people who do their go-between business.

8

The purple shield woman was still trying to fit her luggage in the backseat of the sedan. She got in, bending over, her ass held in hot pink bike shorts. The door slammed as she sat straight, peering out, clocking me. She'd taken off her visor to press her face into the window like a child watching a jail transport bus roll by. Me, the prisoner in the open air. Her, safe in the back there.

Everyone who looked at me—even the Director—came loaded with ideas about me. Fascinated by all the family signifiers, he never noticed the reality. Behind the scenes, fucking what didn't exist. Actress whisperer. Seducing secondhand access. Daughter-of is never lateral. It expands in all directions. Maddening for me that the public version of my parents was made out of *not caring*. Trying to turn away from optics and hierarchies. The cheap refrain from "All Around":

"Power destroys the individual.

Collective sigh."

The van pulled up next to me. On the window, "fuck you" written with a finger in pollen dust. I could see the reflection of a ring stain below the neck of my shirt. Blood and spit in a faded soft puddle. This new double moved aside on the sliding door and I climbed in.

"Margot Highsmith?"

II

This little town outside of New York City where my mother had grown up was far enough away from skyscrapers that there were cows, close enough that there were trains. At first we'd lived with my grandmother Josephine, hid out until the dust settled. Sometimes a photographer would be lurking, eager to revisit it all, to place it at the top of the tabloids again. But, for the most part, no one bothered us. They were more interested in my father than my mother. And me, well, I was only the grand-daughter-daughter-of. I couldn't pretend I wasn't, because I had that very particular birthmark at my hairline. People had been remarking on it from the time I was photographed as a child. Like Jay on the plane.

There were hundreds of these shots online even now, me being carried by my father, my mother ahead of us, just in frame. Once news of their separation and my mother's new romance hit the papers, the attention increased. Then, every single week, I would take the train alone, wearing a red baseball cap, into the city to see my father. I hated trains. My mother had toted me for years, like luggage, all over the continent on her tours.

III

"Margot, come on!" She yelled without turning around. I was sitting on top of a stack of trunks covered in slimy stickers. Josephine had given me a small folder before I left. On one side were sheets of sun-faded sugar paper and a pencil, and on the other five packs of stickers from the stationery store in town. The back of each plastic-wrapped set was a piece of card stock larger than the rest, with a keyhole at the top. At the store, the packs were threaded onto a long, upturned metal rod. There were rows of these slotted into the linoleum strips in front of the birthday cards. I had watched the girl take the rainbow stickers out of a box and angle all fifty packs onto the hook. Not one by one, but all together, with a grin, like she'd won a game.

"Margot, if I turn around and you're putting stickers on the equipment, I swear to God . . ." I had stuck three Easter bunnies outlined in white over a bumper sticker in blood-letting font. I couldn't read so didn't know what it said, but I remember carefully matching the rabbits' ears with the oozy line. Silhouettes of haloed gloss were left where I pulled the stickers off the paper. I had dropped the first three empty sheets on the ground while one of the band workers pushed me through the station. Each had the same figures on it, every pack a repeat story. I had put pastel eggs all over the raised plastic of a funny-shaped guitar case. My mother still hadn't turned around. So, I let the last sheet go, wind litter for the track. And climbed higher up the pile of instruments.

And then I fell.

There was a loud crash as a black textured case hit the concrete. This finally caused my mother to stop walking. The caravan halted behind her, and everyone turned to look. I was on the ground, not far from the edge of the platform. I felt nothing, registered only calm dissonance with the crowd's reaction.

Before anyone could say anything, as my mother lapped the line of assistants, I got up and patted my skirt down. Within seconds she was beside me, pawing at my body. "I'm fine, Mommy." She was embarrassed, concerned about what it looked like to everyone. They pretended to talk to one another and busied themselves loading the racks into the train car ahead.

My mother grabbed my hand without bothering to check under my dress, where I'd fallen on my knees. She pulled me into the front car with her. I weighed too much for her to pick me up as my father did. She was so frail beneath the thick leather jacket and denim shirt. Always in those black boots that made a noise as she strode ahead of me. "Too many trains, too many trains," I thought to no one.

The seats of the train car were covered in rainbow diamond velour like softened stained glass, '80s red, orange, yellow, and purple. I felt nauseous, bent my head, lifted the armrest and tried to burrow into the corner. I was dizzy and the fabric was blending with the throbbing beat in my head. No one else could hear it, I was sure. Triggered by the fabric pattern, some kind of synesthesia. The train car was rumbling but it hadn't pulled away from the station. Every bench outside the windows stood still.

I remember how I hadn't registered the gash in my leg until it bled over. It was my mother's bandmate who noticed it and screamed. The white tulle under my dress had caught red at the edges. The blood through the pink moiré taking a faint shape of woodgrain. "Oh my God, you're bleeding." My mother looked stunned at first, but quickly resolute.

"It's fine. Can you call Joe?" She stood up and pulled tour merchandise from the luggage rack above. "Here, Margot, you wanted one of these anyway." I logged the panic in her shaking hands. Two shirts were stuck together, long sleeves tangled. She became frustrated and handed them both to me. I looked up at her, unsure what to do. I felt nothing but embarrassment, even as the crew medic came to bandage me. He looked worried as he rolled my tiny calf from side to side. I felt only the throb of prying eyes, the same as when I went out with my father or grandfather. Nothing in my leg.

My mother pulled him aside and whispered something in his ear. He looked back at me and I stared at the opposite seat corner. She looked uncertain about something. Her pause to comfort me waited for a response that never came. I didn't want to see it, so I looked down, watched the blood seep along the lines in the silk. I expressed no pain in sound, because I felt none. I didn't yet speak, couldn't explain.

It felt as if all those eyes were seeing something that wasn't there—like the strangers who stopped and stared when I was with my parents. We were just a family. Were once. The medic and my mother looked at me the same way, thinking they knew what I felt because they were familiar with what presented before their eyes.

IV

When I was five, I told my father I wanted to be a beasty-boy. Two words, like a snow leopard, an animal-creature. The Boy part, the Leopard: unsexed.

He laughed. "You should tell people, 'I want to be like Kate Bush when I grow up.' She's a cool girl."

"Who's that? Why not a beasty-boy?" I tried to climb into his lap. "Or an actor, then." When my mother was home, I would sit tightly held between her crossed legs. She liked me to climb up and she'd loop her arms under my knees. Then my feet would dangle and she would hug me close. When I tried this with my father, he always became defensive and hard. Sometimes he would gently lift my hand off his knee and cross his legs the other way. Or he would stiffen, contract the calf muscle that I had edged into, sitting close to him on the floor. In public he always picked me up.

He ignored my questions. "An actress, you mean?"

"What's the difference?"

"In my day—" he stopped himself. "Just be a performer that's already a woman." He looked thrown by what he had just said. I was upset that he questioned my vision.

"Does this Kate Bush do rap?"

"No, she's like your mom, from a fancy family. Does her own thing, very out there. Likes books! She wears those things you wear to dance class?"

"Tutus?"

"No, the tight ones?" He gestured as if choking himself. "You have one in black and—"

"Leotards!"

"Yes, those. You know she trained as a ballerina."

"The Bush lady?"

"Kate, yes."

"How do you know?"

"Your mother knows her. She met her during the summer she was in a band with Björk: Spit and Snot. She was a baby."

"You said snot."

"I did. Then your mother left Iceland and went to London for a few years." He paused and stared at the wall.

"What?"

"Nothing."

"Tell me."

"I just realized something."

"What?"

"You won't understand. Hey, what was your mother saying the other day when you were watching that show?"

"The disappearing one?"

"Yeah, forget it. Um, Kate danced, yes."

I was kicking the wall with my Mary Jane.

"Come here. Get up. Stop that. I will play you a song."

"I'm hungry."

Maybe I wasn't talking loud enough. My father had bad hearing from his years playing large concerts. He hadn't started out that way, but things changed. It seemed like a good idea for my parents not to be in the same band. But this distance created more distance. When my mother was mad at my father, she'd say something under her breath about selling out. He'd get angry and leave the house. One time he had no choice but to come right back in, because there were people with cameras waiting for him outside.

I was at my least invisible when I was next to him, out in the world. People would caw at me, saying how cute I looked. Outside he was attentive, carried me close. Here inside, though, away from the public, that switched over. It was like he didn't see me.

My father got up and swatted my feet out of his way. He went to the painted wooden box he had built for his ancient equipment. The entire floor was poured concrete. Always cold. That's why he wore Moroccan slippers that he kept just by the padded door. The door was lined with rubber, so that it would hold tight to sounds. Keep some in. Keep some out. That day, my father had come home in a sour mood, he had something on his mind, but felt obligated to watch me.

There was a record player to the left, a CD player to the right. I would be punished for days if I touched either of them. The same for the electric piano that he kept stored in the orange box. There were a million knobs to twist on the dashboards of the other equipment, but these didn't interest me so much. I liked the pedals. Sometimes when my father wasn't paying attention, I would try to push one down with my little feet. There was never any sound, as I couldn't reach the switch on the black back wall. All the colored cables and cords.

I liked to sit in the spot just in front of the CD player. Sunlight came through the sky right there. There was a butter-colored leather cushion set up for me. I used to call the shiny round shapes that snapped into their plastic boxes, rainbow-catchers or Disc-os.

"It's on a Disc-o?" My father nodded and handed me its clear jewel box. I pulled out the stapled booklet in the front window. "Why do all of them have this thing? Like a little magazine?"

"Put that back." I held it in my tiny hands and stared at the image on the cover: a porthole to two legs in opaque tights; red satin ballet slippers on white sand. "Kate."

"There's a tear," I said, pointing to the black stockings in the photograph. "Why do they have these magazines?"

"It's old, they don't even make those things anymore. Just put it back in there. I think that one has the lyrics printed inside."

"Lyre-ics?"

"Yeah, like the words to the songs. When me and your mom had The House, we used to spend hours making those. There was one time we did them all by hand. All the words to the songs were in there, because we purpose-fully sang them all crazy. So people had to pause and think, to try to understand. You're good at remembering songs. I've heard you sing—"

"I don't know how to read."

"Right. But you *listen*." My father said this to me often. Bent over on one knee, his right hand placating pain in his back, he settled the silver disc in the plastic tray. It slid in and he flipped the machine shut. There was the sound of shuffling. I had once watched the discs at one of his friend's houses. It had been different; they went in sideways instead of flat. Thin round metal sheets slotted in like a millipede in a back bend, tail to head. The one at our house only had six shallow spots to churn. I lost interest in the music when it started to play, and went for a tumble on the soft cushion.

"Stop that. You're going to hurt yourself."

I put my legs down on the floor. Paused and cocked my head. Concrete in the sunroom. "I like this," I said.

"Your mother loved this song."

"Her friend sings it?"

"Not anymore. Your mother is very difficult."

"Mom's coming home soon, right?"

"She used to have this playing while she made dinner."

"Dad, did you hear me?"

"You take ballet. Show me some moves. We should watch the music video that goes with this." I had started to burrow headfirst, pushing the cushion so that it was no longer in the light. "I said, stop that." He had gotten up to fiddle with some of the wires that I was forbidden from touching. But he didn't know that I had found the plug on the other side, and sometimes stuck guitar picks in the holes. Or I would braid the cables as best I could and hope he'd notice the next day. Little acts of sabotage as gifts.

I lifted my head to see where he had gone and said, "I want to be the girl in movies."

"Yes, an actress?"

"She is all the things."

"All the things?"

"I'm hungry."

"Please, Margot. Wait half an hour." He only looked at me when he heard the pillow slide across the floor. I nudged it again with my Mary Jane. He shook his head and fixated on something outside the back window.

"Look at me!" If I tucked my head in tight enough, I could do a full forward roll and land on my feet.

"Stop! Margot, please. You are going to kill yourself."

"Can you get me some slippers like yours?"

"Sure, what size are you?"

"Don't know."

"Right. I'll ask the nanny."

"You mean Petulia?"

"Yes, your Petulia."

"My Petulia. But she's gone away to Disneyland this week."

"Oh," he looked at me again with a puzzled expression. "You know my father was an engineer there?"

"He drove the train? The modern one?"

He laughed. "Yes, exactly."

"Mom's dad didn't know how to drive."

"How do you know that?"

"She told me. Said he had a driver take him places."

"Ah. He was quite the man."

"Josephine says that, too."

"Oh." And he changed the subject back to music, as he always did. "How do you even know who the Beastie Boys are? That was way before your time."

He could talk for hours about bands and songs, lyrics and instruments, history and melody. Anything to avoid talking about his feelings.

"Josephine lets me watch TV sometimes. She says she wants me to spend more time with her."

"God help you," he said quietly.

"She says that to me, too," I said. He laughed.

"Back to the Beastie Boys. You didn't hear about them from me. Certainly not your mother. Way too mainstream for her."

"They're good. I don't listen to backpack music."

"Backpack music? Do you mean backpack rap? What?" He started laughing. "Where did you learn that?"

"Like that blond girl. My friend likes her songs, and she has a backpack with her face and name on it." He smiled quietly then.

"Ah, so backpack music means you can get the merchandise?"

"Yeah. There aren't any Beastie Boys backpacks. I also like Björk. She doesn't have a backpack. See."

"I can give you some names to impress your mother. And they definitely don't have backpacks."

"Okay."

"It's also okay to like backpack music, you know?" He knelt down a little closer to me. "There were good musicians before your time, and some of them were even on lunchboxes."

"That's silly. No one carries a lunchbox."

"You're right," he said, and stood back up. "Beastie Boys," he repeated, and turned towards the window overlooking Greene Street.

"You said mom's coming soon," I whined. "What's a music video? Can I have a snack?"

My father stepped out of the light and all I could see was his dark profile in relief against the flat view of three windows before the sky. He turned to look at me. It felt strange and I tried to sit up taller. I was ashamed for having expressed any need, even though my stomach was starting to make noises. We stared at each other, speechless, but it only lasted a few seconds and then he patted me on the head.

V

I was twelve when I walked to the fence. There were supposed to be nineteen cows on the property. It wasn't our property, it belonged to my mother's best friend, *childhood* best friend. She didn't speak to her anymore.

I only ever counted nine cows. Why the extra ten were always talked about, I didn't know. I thought city people liked to talk about cows in numbers. Herds. "A group of twelve or more cows is called a flink," Josephine told me. She always liked keeping count of things, slotting them into special words. But this flink didn't add up, and I never knew why she made the fuss. The daughter of my mother's old friend was the only one who ever admitted to me, in a hushed voice, that there were actually only nine. She also taught me not to microwave metal cups.

When I was six, Josephine started to tell me bedtime stories about an actress who used to live not far from where we were. She knew I wanted to be an actress too, and she encouraged it. Josephine and the girl in the story had been best friends. The first night she spoke of her, she told me about a happy, blonde girl who was so beautiful that people told her right from the start she would be a star. I really liked this part.

With every subsequent telling, every time I stayed over, the story darkened. By the time I was eleven, and ready to be done with hearing about her, the girl wound up in an institution where she was badly treated every day for an entire year.

Every night for a month. Every day for a year. Rape wasn't explicit, I figured it out much later. Everything with Josephine was told in days or numbers, in an effort to clock or stop her own body-life. She was seldom affectionate or even attentive at any other time but story time. My grandfather had been a big man. Josephine remained the wife-of, even after he was gone. I understood this too. Hazily, as a teenage girl does, I could always sense him there behind her.

I didn't plan to loiter long by the fence of the house with the missing cows. Josephine's place was down the way, it was bigger, and the floors didn't sound out beneath stocking feet. And while I liked the daughter, I knew my mother would not be happy that I was on enemy land.

My mother often left me with Josephine when she had to go away unexpectedly. She remained leery of my father till after everything had settled down. When I was younger, and she'd just started the new band, she had tried taking me on the road. She would always forget something important, like my headphones for the noise, or food for when there wouldn't be any. Bringing me along was supposed to make her feel better about her choices, but it made things worse for me.

Josephine happily took me in whenever, and even enrolled me in a nearby school, just in case. She was the only one of them who wasn't into making music. A dancer. She worked adjacent to the music, forward-facing but in the background all the same. In all things like an actress, but silent, and not the actual maker of anything but movement. Or maybe this wasn't true, because she made music be seen. She knew everyone's story.

And Josephine had stories to last days. I had heard this whispered about when I was younger, and thought it made sense as she had in every way given birth to our beginning. And she had watched over me full-time since I was nine. Since my mother ran away from domestic life with my father. Josephine always sided with blood. This may have been where the confusion started. I left her behind some days to go to the edge of the field. There were *never* nineteen.

That day, I counted the cows. One two three four five six seven eight. I couldn't find the ninth, and wondered if she too had vanished. There was a break in the electric wire, as if someone had bent the top line one way and the bottom the other. No cow could have gotten through—not even a crow, which explained the iridescent hash on the ground, scalped beak-skull. Josephine said a group of crows was called a murder. I used my foot to grind the remains deeper into the mulch. No spark, no glitter left in the soil.

I heard a sound behind me.

No one was there. No Eight or even Nine. I knew what I was going to do, though I kept telling myself in my head not to do it. Be careful. Remember the fried crow: lit up, ashes of black opal, fat carcass in the grass. I had come close before and what had held me back wasn't a sensation, but a feeling. Two different things. I didn't know they weren't the same then. Somewhere the feeling said not to. It warned my brain based on hammered-in information, notably Josephine telling me, "Stay away from the flink." In my mind, this also meant the wire links. Words can get mixed up and are difficult to unravel when you don't have sensation. I felt plugged, trapped, unable to release something I couldn't explain. Josephine had sensed it that morning as she questioned me. "What will you do today?"

"I don't know."

"Why don't you sit on the porch and paint?"

"I feel heavy."

"Heavy? You weigh one hundred pounds. Please don't start."

"No, it's not a physical thing." I couldn't explain that it wasn't physical in the second sense, but also not about my body.

"I will set up the materials. You will get dressed. Then come down to paint. Or do you want to go into your grandfather's studio?"

"To paint?"

"Certainly not to play the guitar."

"How do *you* know?"

"Watch your tone, young lady."

"I take lessons."

"You do?"

"Yes, from my father."

"Not the greatest guitar player in the world."

"Right, he's ranked twenty-fifth."

"See?"

"You're hopeless."

"Your mother is a better musician."

"You think she's a better everything."

"You're hers, too." It was a strange thing for a grandmother to say. I didn't know if she meant that I was more valuable as my mother's daughter than my father's, or that my value was in belonging at one remove to Josephine. It was painful to sit there trying to decode her riddles as she stared at me. Always a palpable smugness, her chin lifted the tiniest bit too high, so she could look down her perfect little nose.

"Gotta go," I said, without waiting for a response.

It took three minutes to get to the field that morning. In the past when I had timed it on my phone, it was always five or seven. But that day I ran, full of determination. Josephine had not yelled after me. She didn't yell. Ever. That was only for people who were out of control. She was always performing being a human being to her own playbook.

I walked to the break in the fence and placed one palm on each end of the cut wire.

At first I felt nothing. And then came a shiver, like when I would play with my mother's friend's daughter's hair. She and her friends were always playing strange games that let you touch one another in acceptable ways, to create sensations that were not.

That chill. Then, nothing.

And then another shiver, this time in my legs. My feet were always numb, even on the hot sand in summer beyond the touch of the tide. Or when my father, almost drunk, on one of his nights would make me run barefoot in the city snow. I felt nothing then. He would lift his feet like sewing machine pins and they would turn bright pink. I felt nothing. Told no one.

I thought if I touched the wires I would know for certain, but they didn't have much effect. Like when I had put the guitar picks in the electrical socket. Nothing had happened then, either. My mother had freaked out when she heard about it, and I had started crying. That seemed to make her think that I needed her attention. I logged that. And from then on I kept pretending, taking cues from reactions. I mimicked the onlooker's level of intensity. I didn't feel anything when a knife slipped and took a sliver of my finger. My bagel shop boss threw up.

I never understood why other children hated going to the doctor so much, why they cried at shots or the finger prick. I could kick my knee when the doctor hit it with the orange gummy triangle. Sometimes I forgot to, but then he would try it again and I would do it right. I experimented on myself all the time.

I took the two ends of wire, threaded them together and felt something very faint. It began in that hard callus on my left foot and ran to each toe. I braided the two wires more tightly and licked them, closed my eyes and let my mouth fall open, my jaw widen. And for a moment I was outside of my body looking at myself, like that nun statue in the books at the back of the house. Thérèse in a head cloth, a deep hole below stone lips. Like an acting exercise, imagining the sculpture as an extension of myself. I put the wet cables to my chest, as I'd seen one of the coaches do to the dead kid who had been hit at the lacrosse game. My t-shirt was too thick. At least that seemed like a good enough reason. No sensation, but the feeling that something wasn't right.

The defibrillator machine hadn't reset his heart. How often does violence restart life? It was the saddest thing I'd ever seen up until that point. My mother shouted at me afterward: "This is why a middle schooler does not go to a high school sporting event!"

The chances of hitting someone between heartbeats with a ball traveling at 100 miles per hour is almost nil.

What a stupid thing to say.

A diamond-eyed cow made an uncharacteristic bleating noise, and I dropped the wires, turned and ran home.

VI

"She's only thirteen," I heard someone say.

"There are no pyramids here."

"Where is Rose?"

"In the back, weeding." I pulled my bare foot back from where it showed in the doorway.

"I haven't seen her the past few weeks, not even for meals."

"She's in the flower beds."

"Rose lives in the garden."

"It calms her."

"She's better agitated."

"On stage."

"In the world."

"Should be the same, no?"

"Professionalism—"

"— is when they are not the same."

"Not exactly, no."

"Pop stars today shape-shift all the time, online, everywhere. Persona can't match the reality. Bad business. Mass appeal."

"Sincere and always on the margins." Someone coughed. "Play at counterculture, giving nothing back."

"Refuse all."

Or she might have said "refusal," but I became bored and went to the back window to look out at the garden. My mother insisted on cultivating it some strange English way. Different than the other houses far down the freeway, with lawns cut level by electric ride-on mowers every two weeks, with rows of pansies unpotted from black plastic and tuck-patted into holes.

At The House, my house then, there were tall grasses and wild daisies. Ivy grew up all over the stick arches. The flowers were at different heights: purple and blue bells, white lacy discs, red, black, and yellow saucers. There, my mother always wore the same denim shirt tied at the waist over loose jeans. Her hair braided and twisted up on top, and what looked like a metal headband before you saw the foam circles over each ear. Every few beds she would pause to untangle the cord to the player from the weeds.

"What did you write over there?" someone said loudly, to get someone's attention. I looked back towards the room.

"Three-letter things: MI5, KGB, IRA, CCTV."

"Last one is four."

"Who cares."

"Don't get so carried away. We're in rural Michigan."

"Your self-mythologizing is as bad as theirs."

"When does Steve get back?"

"Tomorrow, I think. He said his mother needed some help with curtains at her place."

"It might be time to call it."

"Call what?"

"Everything."

"Before we go . . ."

"Or descend into self-parody, like Jack said."

"Did you watch that movie last night?"

"The Gregory LaCava one?"

"I fell asleep."

The phone that was attached to the wall rang, startling everyone.

"Don't get it."

"Tapped."

"Shut up."

The House was in the suburbs an hour outside of Detroit. My father had found it when he was a teenager, an empty shell for squat parties. No one knew when or how they would happen. But sometimes and somehow they did. The performances were never planned, and only a few were ever documented. The stuff of legend so swiftly.

It's how he first met my mother. She just showed up one day. He said it was love at first sight. She said she ignored him for as long as she could. Everyone else said she knew exactly what she was doing.

I'd overheard parts:

"Rose had her eye on him."

"Guitar prodigy from a working-class neighborhood."

"Steve Highsmith wouldn't be caught dead in Providence."

"He had the one thing Rose couldn't have and she wanted it badly." My mother, at her fancy college where everyone knew about her fancy record-producing father, a close confidant of Mingus.

The conversation at the table continued:

"Does he know?"

"Don't talk about it. Quiet. Let them finish on their own terms."

"Like the band, before we all fall into . . ."

"Self-parody."

"It's time to go."

"Go where?"

"Somewhere else, now that everyone knows *here*."

"But the information network."

"We aren't Baader Meinhof."

"They never called themselves that."

"It's all sincere."

"Not once you say it."

"Steve is operating with an alter ego."

"What?"

"The new group. He's no longer up there himself."

"Rose knows."

"He can't keep this place running without funding."

"But how will we do what we need to?"

My right foot knocked over a stack of books. "What's that noise?" I turned my face away from them.

"What's for dinner?"

"We can figure it out after practice."

"It's Rose's turn."

"When does Steve get back?"

"Don't know. Why?"

"He can't take a two-week holiday from here."

"He's on tour."

"This is his reality."

"This. Not that."

"I meant to tell you: there were crowds of people waiting outside Milan FCI."

"That sounds like a football club."

"Again, this is rural Michigan."

"FCI is Federal Correctional Institution."

"They wanted someone out?"

"No, they wanted to show solidarity with someone who was in."

"Oh."

"Yeah, very confusing."

"Everything is confusing."

VII

When I returned to Josephine's I found some big unopened envelopes that she had left on my bed. There must have been a dozen uniform envelopes, some discolored. I checked the postage dates; they had been sent years ago. All were from the same agency, the one my grandmother had called back when I first mentioned wanting to be an actress. I remembered the three letters in its name. It was the biggest one, with a music division *and* a film division. She'd made one call, and something had happened. Then she'd fought with my mother. No one had ever explained any of it to me. I tore into the packages.

I told my mother that I wanted to drop out of school sophomore year, but she wouldn't let me. I told my father and he said he'd think about it. My whole life this weird double bind. People talk about algorithms versus actuarial science, but it's nice to think that either one exists in personal life. Having separated parents makes the feedback loop more confusing: two parents who strangers know, one much more than the other, makes it very difficult.

When they give you advice, each aware of the other, are they asking you to make reparations for their past? That's how I always felt it was with my mother. For both her past and my childhood, and then for what happened, and what would happen.

I looked at the first page of one of the scripts and recognized the title of a children's movie I'd recently seen a post about. Some of them were so old that they'd already been made. I felt angry.

"Josephine," I yelled. I could hear that two-step rhythm of her feet on the stairs, then in the hall. Her face at the door, her bangled arm bent.

"Yes, I've been saving them. You were too young. Let them think you're picky. I responded to all the follow-ups, don't worry."

"Of course you did."

"Watch your mouth. It's not my fault—your mother forbade it."

"Why do I not believe you?"

"You're still a minor."

"I'm sixteen, almost seventeen."

"Still too young to be jetting off and abandoning school."

"I missed weeks at a time whenever I was—"

She interrupted. "It would have been too confusing for you. Stability now. No more new locations and strange crews."

"But that's why I wanted to be an actress in the first place."

VIII

For the next year, Josephine would ferry me to sanctioned auditions in the city and back. I was supposed to read the scripts sent by the agency and then submit them to her with my character's lines highlighted (in yellow only). There was a mint-green metal tray on her desk where I had to leave them once I was done. If she approved, she would send a few emails, find out the days and times of the audition. If she knew the director or casting agent or someone who did, she'd arrange a phone call. This would generally lead to a dinner. Table for three. Josephine would never let me go alone.

"Are you ready, Margot?"

"I've been ready."

"Did you change your outfit?"

"No."

"Well, we're not going. You can't wear that to meet him."

"Then I'm not going."

"Your loss." Josephine wanted me to wear one of her old silk blouses, with tiny matte diamonds all over and a pie crust collar. A pair of black suiting pants, not new either, had been left next to the blouse on my bed. She had quizzed me for days about the character, a show-jumping sophomore in boarding school. How would she talk? What would she want? What mistakes would she repeat over and over? What would the girls be saying behind her back? It was an effective exercise; it worked most every time.

I took off my jeans and t-shirt and put on the blouse, unhooking the silk loops at the wrists so my hands could fit through. The lace outline of my bra showed through the thinning silk. There were riding boots at the end of the bed. I had no idea where she'd found them or how she knew my size.

"Margot."

"Yes, I'm coming." I ran down the stairs, my feet sliding forward in the boots.

"Let me look at you," she said. She was wearing her gold choker with the red ruby in the middle. The diamonds on my blouse matched the tinkling thin shapes hanging fringe-like from the choker. I threw my arms in the air, striking a pirouette pose.

"I like that necklace."

"It belonged to the wife of one of your grandfather's friends, big jazz man. When she picked me up, I was wearing an old black unitard. She took it off her neck and insisted, told me to keep it, said it reminded her of a bad night long ago."

I put my hands on my hips and looked at her. "That doesn't worry you? It's cursed."

She laughed loudly. "I decide what's cursed."

"She was your friend."

Josephine didn't respond. Her honey-colored hair was dried straight. She wore a black suit with a shirt unbuttoned beneath it, the collar touching the sun spots on her clavicle. Her left wrist was covered in gold hinged bangles. If you snuck a peek at her jewelry box, you would find everything in rows, cataloged by provenance.

"Do you need to bring the script?"

"It's not an audition."

"In case it comes up."

"I have it memorized."

"Remember, she's a girl from the South, not New England."

"Like you."

She ignored this too. Her accent had disappeared long ago. "Bring a bag with a change of clothes. We may end up staying at the apartment." It was a Thursday. The apartment was my grandfather's *pied à terre*: the third floor of 208 East 13th Street.

On the train ride into the city, Josephine kept her legs crossed to the man beside her and her gaze out the window. I sat across from her and tried to read a book I had been assigned for English class. She had brought some book a friend had written. A kid walked by and looked me up and down. He asked me if I'd missed my stop last century. I laughed. My grandmother smiled without showing her teeth.

We were supposed to meet this director who Josephine knew through a friend, at a restaurant on West Broadway at 8 p.m. I had been briefed that he was coming from shooting something in Central Park. He was already there, in a tennis shirt and sneakers. I clocked his red running pants when he stood up as we arrived at the table. My grandmother, wise that I was about to make a joke, gave my hand a squeeze. I remained silent.

"Josephine, it's so good to see you. I don't think we've set eyes on each other since George's funeral."

"I think you're correct," she said, sitting down beside him and pointing me to the chair opposite. "This is Margot, she's very excited to meet you."

"*Enchantée*," I said. Josephine glared at me. We all sat down. When I ordered a tequila on the rocks she glared at me again. Soon she was on her second martini. The director had a drink to match each of hers. She would never get drunk, though. She was never out of control. The skill was in taking other people there.

We didn't talk much about the movie. He would try to bring it up and my grandmother would bend the conversation back to something more mundane. We had spent so much time prepping the character; I didn't understand this tactic. She would glare at me three more times throughout the meal. The director relaxed into himself and his martinis, chuckling at her stories about when she filled in as a back-up dancer for an awards show a few years ago. She had been nearing fifty. The meal dragged on past dessert and so did her stories. She had stopped drinking, he had not. I had seen this happen many times before, but I only realized it then: it wasn't that Josephine loved a long night, a good time. It was that she would never end a good time before it was clear that she was the one who'd made it happen.

IX

There was a span of seven months during my junior year when my mother tried her hand at being domestic, which simply meant existing in the same city and house as me, morning and evening. She started to wear a bandana tight around her neck, like the other mothers with their silk scarves. None of them accepted her; they all knew who she was. High school in reverse, the cool kid forever outcast. An outsized mystique meant you had no need of community.

My mother was rarely invited to dinner parties or cocktails. A girl once told me she'd overheard her own mother say, "Don't invite Rose. She's single now. She'll flirt with your husband." My mother didn't want their doctor husbands. I could have assured them of that. What she did like was attention, an arm's-length seductive haze. She always said she didn't like the lenses, the headlines, the stares. But this was because she liked to refuse them. The riddle my father could never solve was how to maintain, and tend to, this state of perpetual denial.

In her early days in the band, at my father's side, the town loved her as one of their own. When she defected, leaving him and everyone else behind, they turned their backs on the direction she left in. And then there was me. She left as one and came back as two, not three: without him and with me. PTA and class trips didn't interest her. They never put her on the list; they called it an oversight, but there were oversights galore. This must have hurt her, for though she wouldn't have wanted to attend, she wouldn't have wanted to be unwanted.

A big withholder, she was never affectionate towards me, but I sensed her behind my eyes as I fell asleep. No handholding, no cuddling, but she would stay and stare. And I started to feel safest like that. Being watched in places that weren't my own, as people that weren't me. An actress.

I rarely invited men—or boys, as they were back then—to come over, because I never liked anyone to see my personal space, to know anything of my home life. This may have come quite arrogantly from having famous parents, the celebrity other kids wanted to access; not my time, or my few age-appropriate toys. I kept personal details and objects hidden, because of that time when a girl came over and stole one of my father's cassette tapes.

She did it like no one would know or care, as if no one was going to miss a piece of ancient technology. And the strangest part was I watched it go down, convinced of her villainy but unable to intervene. How she asked to use the bathroom after casing my place. She went straight into the den and spent five, ten minutes snooping. Meanwhile it was clear to all of us. We sat there on the concrete floor, in a five-point satanic circle, drinking and playing with our phones. The girl came back with the front pocket of her hoodie heavy. I got up and went to the den. Everyone downed a drink.

It was month three of the shoot and I had to go to the set every day. I had gotten the part way back when Josephine had taken me to dinner. There had been two callbacks and I'd worn the same outfit each time. She had seen the director for dinner twice more, too. The movie was filming in the city, and I wanted to move there for the duration, but Josephine said no. Not yet. Her timeline. We practiced the lines every day in my Southern accent.

Without knowing I had already signed up, my mother fought hard to get me to turn it down. This was in my grandmother's office, weeks after it was settled, but she had been away and missed that bit. I told her I could do my schoolwork online. "If I stay, will you promise to stay?" I asked her, and she knew exactly what I meant. And I knew this was my way out.

I saw Josephine watching us through the window in the door. The room like a detective's office in a noir film. She had scratched my grandfather's name on the glass. "Look, I have to go grocery shopping," my mother said.

"Really?" I asked. She rolled her eyes and left me there in front of the computer. The thing she didn't understand was that it was easier at home when she wasn't around. I wouldn't have to wonder about her state of mind, worry I might say something to upset her, something apparently harmless; she was easily set off. Her love for me was the same as her love for my father, which had been either all in or all out depending on what he stoked within her that day or how everyone else was seeing him. The everyone else was conditional on who she wanted to listen to. Some days Josephine was all the everyone Rose needed, an oracle licensed to make judgments and plans; forever plotting.

"Margot," Josephine said, having come closer, grown larger in the window frame, her hands still somehow small. "I will drop you off on set. We leave at six a.m. tomorrow." I hadn't even looked at the week's call sheet. She'd gotten hold of it somehow. I was still a minor, she would remind me. One of her bracelets had worked past her elbow and was wedged above the bone. "What's wrong with your finger?" she asked, eyes narrowing behind the glass.

"I burned it on the stove making pasta earlier." I knew it looked offensive to her. A boil that was filled up, hard. It made the rhythm when I typed on the keyboard different than usual. Josephine said nothing and started to head towards her bedroom, stopped and walked back. "Be more careful, Margot. This is not the first time this has happened." I nodded. She left.

I opened the desk drawer. There was a plastic container of tacks inside. I took one and glanced round to make sure no one was watching. Then I pushed it into the boil which exploded fluid all over the "K" key. It was flat now, all one surface and I tore off the dead deflated skin, sent the email I had been writing, and left the study to prepare for the following day.

When I got upstairs, I saw my mother in the bathroom, wiping her eyes with a hand towel. I could see her jeweled cigarette case balanced on the edge of the tub, fastened shut. And as if knocked by an unseen hand to alert her I was there, the silver case slipped abruptly into the bath making a loud noise, part metal on porcelain, part pill maraca. I knew the tiny beats within the larger one, assorted medicines, "vitamins." She dropped the towel and turned, not toward the noise, but to meet my eyes through the doorway. And then, before either of us had time to assess the damage, she slammed the door shut.

X

Josephine softened in my senior year, once I was admitted to the college she had chosen. It was the same one my mother had gone to. She was possibly too credentialled to hold the kinds of unrefined political views people knew her for. But, of course, no one knew *that* for years. In the days when her fame first bloomed, it was easier to keep history hidden, amplifying only what served you. Still, secret legacy admission or not, I was expected to go. It would be common knowledge in my case, of course. But no one bats a bemused eyelid when the child-of-famed-punk-dissident enrolls. It's expected.

My father was the one who strangers would accost, back when we were still all together, out and about in the world. I always thought this bothered my mother, for reasons she denied. Yes, it bothered her. Not because she was jealous, but because something about the way my father had drawn this attention was wrong.

It seemed suspicious that she left him behind only once everyone knew she'd gone there. Once her name had been big for long enough to register solo. Her past had become conveniently hazy around the time he came along. Of course, she could never fully shake the other shade that followed her: being the daughter-of. But her father was a jazz musician and that was, well, classic. It aged well, like my grandmother.

Josephine had tried her best to help me with homework when I was younger. She was not very good at math or spelling, but her confidence carried her over the gaps. It occurred to me that this could be where the cow miscount started. No one dared to question her. So when she told me I'd have to go there, where there was an auditorium named after my grandfather's family—another fact allowed to grow hazy—I couldn't argue. I wrote a terrible essay in a bid to sabotage the process, but this pact had been ratified before I was born. "America," my grandmother sometimes said in her even tone, equal parts awed and mocking.

Once the acceptance came, Josephine calmed down. I think I saw her face relax, which was physically impossible. She was the one who had refreshed the browser while I hid in the bathroom upstairs, painting my toenails on the edge of the bath. She gave a yelp when it came through, as if she had cause to be surprised. It startled me and there was a loud bang, because I slammed my foot against the tub, printing five tiny red squares on the white porcelain.

"Margot, get down here." That one note, never raising her voice.

"I'm busy, what?"

"I'm not going to ask you twice, it will spoil—"

"I'm coming," I yelled, pulling my right leg up onto the other one crossed on the swiveling desk chair. The excess momentum swung me around and the top of my foot hit the bath again. Then I put both legs down and my feet landed hard, stop motion. "I'm coming."

I ran down the wooden stairs and towards the studio room with its windowed doors, I knocked on the glass, and she waved a hand for me to come inside. She didn't look up, but remained squinting over the laptop.

Midday, after her scotch, she'd open the computer to answer emails and send some. She wrote them the same way one would on stationery cards, the same as when she text-messaged: "Very best, Josephine." It wasn't her given name, which is why she always had to remind herself.

I tried to push open the door. It was locked, so I twisted the handle till it rattled and she finally looked up. Her eyes rolled into the back of her head and she stretched out an arm crowded to the elbow with gold bangles. She flicked her wrist outwards, turning the knob clockwise. I went in.

"You got accepted to Brown." I refused to meet her eyes.

"Wow." I stared at the floor, fixating on the messed-up polish of my toes.

"Aren't you happy?"

"Thrilled."

"Acting class hasn't started yet. What is your problem?"

"Did you tell Mom?"

"Of course."

"Cool, I would have let *me* do that if I was *you*."

"What?"

"Doesn't matter. I'm going back upstairs."

"Don't you want to see?"

"I trust you. Even though I can't remember giving you my password." She ignored this and slid one of the bangles up over her elbow in that nervous way she had.

"Okay. Well, your mother is coming home to celebrate with us before you have to go to your father's."

"You can't be serious? I don't want to deal with her."

"Have some respect. She's the reason you got in."

"Dad . . ."

"Yeah, he's not the reason you got in."

"Why are you so cruel about him?"

"I don't remember," she said. This made me think about the stash of notebooks I'd hidden in a cupboard where, until last year, I'd made notes on things. Not just anything, but slights. Also kindnesses. I wrote it all down so I would remember, because my mother had told me to always be cool, never let them know you know. And this had gotten very confusing.

My father had the opposite approach. He said that when someone shows you who they are, you move away. Sever. Be civil, but sever. It was hard to do this as a teenager. There are only so many people in your tiny world and you don't have the ability to create a life outside it. My father never understood that I was a child. I couldn't *leave*. He and my mother left all the time, off on tour somewhere. And when they left each other, the only recourse I had was to pretend the severing was my doing.

So, I logged infractions in the notebooks my grand-mother bought me because she thought they were for running lines and transcribing song lyrics. Ever since that day with my father when he showed me the booklets that went with the CDs, I had started to write down the words to songs. There were websites for this, but I liked doing it myself. There was a meditative quality to it, to pause and listen over and over and translate this onto paper, into words. I felt like I was finally solving something. The notebooks: half lyrics, half behavioral observations. Analog playlists: songs chosen to suit moods.

Josephine, in saying she didn't remember why she harbored such distaste for her former son-in-law, was an example of the kind of person I feared most. The original example. Such people made up their minds and then it was permanent, void of value in real time. There was *nothing* he could have done to make her see him differently. He never had a chance. It was decided before he arrived.

That was also why I didn't want to see the admission email. My grandfather, he of the auditorium, had been some kind of honorary music or arts professor thing there. I hadn't applied anywhere else. My grandmother took great pleasure in this boldness. She had never gone to college, just danced. Danced her way into power, married a few men, and danced some more. In whichever order.

"Okay, Josephine," I said, patting her frail back. "I'm going to go upstairs now and repaint my toenails."

"You better be ready for dinner at eight. Your mother should be here by then. She said J. wasn't coming, he was recording in the city."

"Cool." I opened the door and shut it quietly behind me, leaving her staring at the computer screen in satisfaction.

Instead of going upstairs, I went out the front door. There was a pair of my sandals waiting. I had two hours to get through before I'd be tortured by both of them. I knew that now that I'd officially gotten in, it wouldn't matter so much what I did, so long as my grandmother could reach me on my cell. I always picked up when she called, and this pleased her immensely. I expected her to soften even more over the next few days, then I'd be free to disappear with my boyfriends. And when my mother was out of town again she could take all the pills she wanted and not worry about us.

What bothered Josephine about her daughter's addictions was that she thought people would blame them on her own behavior. She had been a *good* mother and was a *good* grandmother. I let her believe this. But there was a different story in one of the many notebooks.

Although I longed for Manhattan, I liked to walk around by myself in town, along those winding roads with little to see but trees. A city was where I knew I would end up, in Los Angeles or New York. Everyone wants to go to the big city. Why never the reverse? What if I wanted to be exiled one day, willingly banished to some remote wilderness? I thought about that sometimes, the other path, the one that pointed backwards. And then I worried that if I thought about it too much it would come true.

So, I focused on other things. One mile down the road was the house of a friend, and the other way led to the cows. A flink and a murder. If I went to see the cows I might be tempted by the fence, but of course nothing would happen. Not like that poor fried crow. A fence, a rainstorm, some alchemical glitch? But me, I never felt a thing.

Someone drove by in a Camaro blaring music and honked the horn, hung out the window screaming the name of my father's band. At first I thought I'd forgotten to cover the birthmark with a baseball cap, and was set to applaud their laser vision, but then I realized I was wearing some old merch. They had reacted to a t-shirt.

The alarm on my phone went off and I turned around. Hit the screen after it saw my face. It was not worth pressing on with my walk and missing dinner. The cows could wait. Best not be making trouble too soon. Part of my plans always came back to the notebook theory. Keep it all, okay, but know the coordinates. Who and what and when, on standby, till you're ready to truly disappear.

XI

"Do you want another slice?" my father asked. He had set up a folding table and two chairs on the tiny balcony overlooking downtown.

"I don't really eat pizza."

"You polished that off."

"Yeah, well I was starving. I hadn't eaten anything since yesterday."

"Why?"

"I drove straight to F.'s family's apartment in the East Village and we hung out and never thought about food."

"Code."

"*Dad.*"

"Why doesn't he ever want to come here and meet me?"

"He asks all the time."

"What's the problem?"

"I'm not ready. He knows who you are without having met you. That's weird enough. I want to keep things separate for now."

"Whatever you want. You should have told me you don't like pizza."

"Were you gonna cook?"

"I was gonna order sushi."

"Oh yes, that's more like it."

"You want to call?"

"Nah, it's cool. Next time."

"When are you coming back?"

"I thought I'd come before I leave for school. You don't need to come. I was planning on driving there alone."

"You can take the train to Providence, you know? Easier once you get there and are established."

"I don't like trains."

"I got you something as a gift to celebrate."

"Celebrate what?"

"College admission. First, you want a drink?"

"We're drinking together now?"

"Yes." He got up and opened the sliding door. I watched him through the glass make another martini, doubling the measurements this time. He poured a second one, carried them back out the door and to the table.

"Cool. Do you mind if I smoke."

"Roll me one."

"Lol."

"What?"

"Never mind."

"Okay."

I tore off a sheet of rolling paper and flattened it against the table. I could see crumbs poking up from underneath. "Gross, can I clean off this table?" I got up and went to the kitchen to look for a paper towel.

"Sorry, I just put it out for us and ate a bagel on it before.

There are bleach wipes on the shelf." We were used to this dance of getting up and sitting down, the rolling and wiping and drinking and ignoring anything else was new.

When I came back, he had rolled the cigarette I'd left there. He lifted it and flicked off the table with the back of his hand. I started wiping the ring by his elbow.

"So, do you want your gift now?"

"Can I drink a little first." I wasn't asking a question. I caught my reflection in the dirty window, the white-blond part of my hair mottled with grains of whatever it was that had lodged there. "Why don't you have your cleaning lady do the windows?"

"I like it a little gritty."

"Haha." I took a sip and then decided I might as well down it in one go.

"Jesus, Margot."

"*Your* daughter."

"Okay, stay right there."

"Where am I going to go?"

"Dunno." He got up and this time left the door open. I watched him go down the hall and heard him on the stairs of the duplex. A door slammed and then he appeared again with something in his arms. He stopped in the kitchen to make two more martinis. He brought them over, balancing one in each hand. He always wore dress shoes even inside. Old, battered ones, like he couldn't let himself be refined even at home. The Moroccan slippers had gone long ago.

He had on a pair of old suiting pants, with a white t-shirt and a button-down thrown on top. "You're still here. Take these," handing me the drinks, then he walked back in to pick up the package. "Here you go. I got them in Milan when I played a special gig at Cox18."

"Lol, gig."

"Sorry, show." He put the plastic bag on the table. "Look." I reached inside and pulled out an old pair of pink satin pointe shoes with white ribbons. Worn, used. "From Porselli, original ones. Like the Kate Bush album. I looked for red, but—."

"They're cool." I didn't really understand what he was talking about, but he seemed convinced.

"Do you love them?"

"Love," I lied. The last time I'd gone on pointe, someone had to signal me to stop, because my shoes had soaked through. My mangled toes would sometimes bleed until the pink turned red. Like with my princess dress on the train. "Thank you, they are beautiful."

"I didn't know your exact size," he said.

XII

"Lucy, turn down the music."

"Haha, you hate this song."

"You would too if you were me."

"*Everyone* loves this song."

"Twelve people."

"Your dad's a legend."

"Half dead."

"Margot!"

I got up and pushed the button on her screen. "Silence."

"You need quiet to do drugs?"

"*Do* drugs. Oh my God, who are you?"

"Margot."

"Stop saying my name. Please, just a little quiet for a minute."

"Is it hard to unscrew the bottle with your pills?"

"*Very.*"

"I'm a little worried about you," Lucy said.

"There's nothing to be worried about." I swallowed two of the small, hatched tablets. "I come from a long line of addicts. Of all kinds."

"That's the problem."

"And *they*'re all still alive!"

"Alive is relative. Remember when Rose said life for her has always been about palliative care."

"Depression runs deep. I love that you call her Rose. That day was awful. I can't even talk about it."

"She told me to!"

"To call her Rose? Yeah, she really likes you."

"We bonded that time at your grandfather's place in the city."

"When?"

"Freshman year, winter break. You had that little party?"

"Oh, yeah."

"I met Josephine, too."

"Right. That's when you were with that guy who was obsessed with old episodes of *The Wire*."

"Most TV guys are."

"Fetishizing the Other. What was his name? Luke? Ted?"

"Chris, the same as my dad."

"That's right. I think that's what attracted you to him."

"Yeah. I think my dad is what attracted him to me."

"Fuck the daughter of who you want to be. Very American merit-oc-racy."

"We've talked about this . . . so much."

"Still holds up. I can't believe I'm turning twenty tomorrow."

When I said that, Lucy shot up from the edge of her bed, knocking two pillows to the floor. Her sheets were bright white with thumb-width salmon stripes. Her towels matching, with scalloped salmon trim. She went over to the Formica armoire, opened it and the hinge parted, dropping the door sideways. A pile of linens fell out. She kicked them aside and reached for something up high. "What are you doing?"

"I'm looking for where I hid the package my mother sent for you."

"She sent me something?"

"Yes, you know she loves you too."

"I only met her that one time we went to your house in the woods."

"Special delivery from Montana," Lucy said as she handed me the package. It was still in the box from the post office, addressed to me c/o L.S. James.

"I can't believe she sent something."

"Open it."

I tore off the landscape edge of cardboard. Inside was a black sweatshirt and something else that fell onto the floor. I held the shirt up to my chest. Lucy started laughing. I tilted my head to read the letters in the facing mirror. They were white, printed in cheap souvenir font: "God Loves Me and There's Nothing I Can Do About It."

"Your mother is hilarious. Dark comedic genius."

"Only you two. I think she found that on the internet. There's a book, too." I looked down to the floor. The cover was yellow, with the photo of a woman wearing a black hair ribbon in front of a tiger cage.

I said, "You always get along better with other people's parents."

"Like grandchildren and grandparents, but there should be another word for it. You would have *loved* my dad."

"I feel close to him for some reason: through you. All those movies we've watched."

"Do you think I should drop out and go into landscape design?"

"Is that a joke?"

"Kind of, but it does seem appealing. Did you know Kropotkin was born a Russian noble?"

"You sound insane. Where is this coming from?"

"I was thinking about when your mom came to visit and told us about the garden she used to keep at that commune place when you were young."

"Your mind just skips from thing to thing. I love it. Sometimes I think I know how it gets there. But sometimes it's a mystery even to me."

"A curse."

"For you. A gift for me. Especially when it comes to other people. I don't know anyone more psychologically astute. A gift, really."

"Two gifts for you!" The phone rang. "Is that the landline? Where the fuck even is that?'

"Sounds like it's coming from the cabinet."

"Oh yes, I put it in there. Must be a mistake. No one ever calls."

Then my cell phone rang. "Hello? . . . Yes. Okay, I'll come now." Lucy cocked her head to one side. "It's the dean's office. They said they called my room and my dumbass roommate told them to call yours and then we didn't pick up . . ."

Her face fell abruptly. "What?"

Two hours later I was on a train to rehab. Or so they told anyone who asked.

XIII

I never went back to school.

I was kicked out. But that's hard to claim when some might say I should never have been admitted in the first place. I didn't go down on the grounds of any academic inadequacy, only my weakness for illegal things. It seemed important to them not to show their miscalculation to the public. I had been let in because of appearances and connections, and so to leave loudly would be taking that credibility with me.

It's okay for kids of musicians to be addicts, it's not one of those things expected to skip a generation. I had been doing well, but even so, they like to factor in a few drop-outs. Never draw attention to what's a fault in the stars. So off I went, quietly. No one made a fuss. I just disappeared one day. They told me they would arrange for my things to be sent wherever they needed to go. Lucy volunteered, agreed to pack everything. And it was then that she first offered her family's place. It was a house I'd been to once, where her father liked to go work. Watch, criticize, and later, write films, far away in Montana. I said no thank you.

Let's save that for when the real problems start. She'd laughed and lovingly untacked my posters from the wall, winding them up tight. Rolling them into a tube.

I had made them all myself, some from scans of old magazines, others were copies of posters I'd found in an abandoned mall shop, where you could flip through the fan of hinged windows. I liked the '80s computer graphics, and sometimes, less sincerely, the pop band ones. It's weird how kids of a certain age recycle these styles and personalities while trying to figure out their own. There were always the models too, different than the musicians: mute body-symbols, most often too skinny, hard to look away. I liked having things around that were unlikely-dangerous.

Someone had reported me for keeping drug paraphernalia in my room. I had found that stuff in my mother's pantry, brought it up to school, and never even used it.

I set *myself* up.

I had also stolen the jeweled cigarette case my mother always carried with her. I didn't smoke, but stored assorted pills in it like she had, so they would rattle around and avoid the lint in my bag. There were two emeralds by the click lock, one hadn't been smoothed, to fit the housing. In the middle, a shallow dish of silver where a diamond once presided between a pair of hammered fronds curling upwards, like question marks knocked on the cupped side. Rows of grooves, like hard wales of corduroy, covered the bottom. It could have been an oversize flip-up lighter, but you had to unlatch it and the hinge was on the back. The hot pink Benadryl tablets looked toxic in the dark interior. I wonder what else she had once carried there.

The bottles of painkillers were another thing. I noticed I didn't react to them like other people did. All they did was clear, and then muddy, passing thoughts in musical form. But I liked them, the way people like gummy bears. They were easy to take from Josephine's medicine cabinet when I was visiting. All the bottles stamped in my mother's name. She kept them there when they'd expired, like stale packaged snacks in the pantry.

The whole incident gave me what I always wanted, to find a fast track, to be free in the city, New York or Los Angeles. I'd never wanted Providence.

"God Loves Me and There's Nothing I Can Do about It."

Controlled changes in environment. A script to follow. Josephine had called it long ago.

New York City was bad punishment.

I had been doing great, even if I was failing biology, which is the most ironic part of a very fucked-up story. Then, some snitch brought my drug tackle (like that stolen cassette tape long ago, another family heirloom?) to the attention of the administration and I obtained what I'd always wanted: an exit.

The administration felt bad about it, so they said I could write my thesis remotely and still graduate. Performance Studies.

It all happened very quickly, and then Josephine called and calmly told me to come to hers. I knew that would make it harder to leave again. So I said, no, mail me the keys to the city place. She said there were tenants. And I said they would have to leave unless she wanted me going straight to Montana. My brattiness made her act fast. I moved into 13th Street.

I arrived with my old Jeep, which I had to park over on 12th Street, and a backpack of clothes. The garage was the same place as Josephine's storage unit. It still contained one of my grandfather's pianos and an assortment of brass instruments in black plastic cases, the insides lined with red or purple flock. And crate after crate of records. I'd gone in there one time to dig around. When Josephine found out she texted me:

"Please don't do that again. I am happy to tell you whatever you need re: your grandfather's estate. Just ask. xJosephine."

I was careful not to make eye contact with the attendant, knowing he was team Josephine. It was a short walk to the apartment. I entered and headed immediately for the big silver fridge.

The woman who had been renting the place had left a fridge full of "natural" energy drinks, flower-petaled goat's cheese rounds, and open Diet Cokes. The one closest to the left was full to the top; to the right, a sip remained. A wave of emptiness like the logo on the bottle.

There was a mattress on the floor like in a Paris apartment, and three potted plants. No curtains, no sheets. Two stained pillows. Beside them, a daybed with a table that jutted out sideways, shaped like a guitar pick. I put my backpack on it and it toppled over. I left it that way when I walked outside to visit the bodega around the corner.

Every time I'd passed by over the years, there had been a black cat with two different color eyes. One white, one yellow. In the center of both, a black oval bigger than the usual diamond slit. The last time I'd seen her had been nearly ten years ago. She was unlikely to still be alive.

People in the street were looking at me strangely, as if they'd noticed someone new in town, one amid the hundreds of others. I was wearing a baseball cap to hide my hairline and big black sunglasses I'd found on the counter by the door. I was moving among everyone in a strange choreography, as someone who'd just been set free. All limbs and music playing in my head. No white plastic earphones, only a smug grin, hands deep in pockets. I sloped up to the deli and tugged open the decal-covered door. A small black cat slid out. Its eyes were different colors, but with the slit instead of the oval, so I knew it was a relative who'd lost out in the genetic lottery. Two generations, three even. Same. There's a pair of us in it, I thought.

"Do you have cigarettes?"

"Of course, what do you think this is?"

"I don't see them."

"They aren't on display anymore."

"I see." He handed me a pack of American Spirit and took off his mirrored glasses; I watched him fold their neon-green hinged arms in and out.

"How did you know?"

"I always know."

"Do you own this shop?"

"My family, yes. For a long time."

"Do you know where there's a good coffee shop around here?"

He laughed. "No one ever asks that. What do you mean?"

"Like a real East Village place."

"Everywhere is real?"

"Right." I swiped my card and took the cigarettes with my other hand. The cat came back in through the take-out coffee window. Its tail tangled for a second in the tubing of one of the bongs on display. "What's the cat's name?"

"Miles Davis."

"Cool," I said and left.

XIV

There was no doorman at my grandfather's place. So I thought I'd be coming and going as I pleased, without worrying about reports back to Josephine. I found out later that she had access to all the cameras.

That day after I bought the cigarettes, I thought maybe I'd go to the park far down East. But it had gotten chilly and by Broadway, I was blowing vapor ahead of me. I turned back. On the opposite curb was a young couple facetiming on one phone with someone, like new parents looking into their child's crib. The person on the other end spoke in a loud baritone. I could hear him all the way across the street. When he yelled something, they looked at me and we all nodded at one another. I went the other way, put my head down and hands back in my pockets. Once across, I pulled out the keys. Three more blocks and I was back on 13th Street. Up the steps, fiddling for the right key, a bit of shaking, then the click-over.

There was a new pile of mail, mostly fat rectangular envelopes rising to a heap on the floor; I kicked them aside. Pushing my hands deeper holding the key, I could see its shape poking to the fore. The back of my pants dragged up each stair, weighing me a little backward as I climbed to the third floor. We owned all the apartments in the building, but this was the one the family stayed in. The door was slightly ajar, and I could see movement inside. Flashes of white and tiny noises, smell of bleach. The cleaning person must have come by to rotate the sheets upstairs and down when the short-term tenants left. A little too late to check on me for Josephine. Her friend who'd been staying there in the family base had hoped to remain, but my grandmother had negotiated early vacancy. Through the door frame, I could see the bed on the floor was covered in a fresh white sheet, new pillows gleamed. Something simmered on the stove.

"Hello?" I walked in and patted the door closed behind me. I felt like an intruder and walked slowly to the next room, turning my head from side to side.

"Margot!" A tiny, white-haired woman ran out. I screamed. She threw her arms around my neck. I had to stop myself from pushing her away.

"Camille?" I realized.

"You remember me?"

"Of course. I—I just wasn't sure—"

"That I was still alive?"

"No, I mean, that you would be here today."

"I'm always around for the changing of the guard. Your grandmother lets me know all the coming and goings."

"I'm sure."

"Do you need anything?" She was looking at the pack of cigarettes half out of my pocket. I had left my backpack on the counter.

68

"No, thank you. I'm all good."

"I threw away the soda and cheese. I started to make tea."

"Thanks."

"You have my number if you need me?" She could tell I didn't want to talk, that I'd expected to be alone.

"I don't think so." I hadn't had a cell phone the last time she'd seen me.

"Put this in: 206-577-9176."

"Cool. Where's that?"

"Small town, Pacific Northwest. You'll probably never go there in your life." She gave me another hug and left through the front door. I noticed she was wearing a designer dress that I had once seen in a photo of my grandmother. She had worn it belted at the waist with a gold cord.

I took my shoes and pants off and lay down on the bed on the floor. It felt good to be there by myself, but I didn't know what would come next. I had an audition set up for that Saturday. Josephine was considering allowing me to change my last name. I told her I wanted to carry on her legacy, which was, of course, what would attract her to the idea of my leaving Margot Highsmith behind.

"Cult enough," the agent had said at first. Though they wanted people to know I was my father's daughter. My grandmother argued that I didn't need to worry about the important people knowing. That the handful of decision-makers knew already. As if the big moves happened in some castle she'd already conquered.

"*Cult enough*" should have rang as the warning it was. I should have heard "important" as an insult.

I knew from a young age that there are two kinds of fame, and you can process this however you want. One kind opens the door to the other, but if you pass through, it will close behind you. This impossibility of return is scary. My father told me about his friends in this band with a name I can't remember. A tale of punk ethics.

They owned their own sound system, charged $5 for entrance, and kept an envelope full of money on stage to give to anyone who misbehaved. A swift refund and a "Get out," if they weren't cool. Some big record guy with a name I also can't remember came to their show in New York and offered them a million dollars.

They said no.

After that the band broke up, because where do you go from there. And two of them came to live with us at The House.

I was born nine years after my father started his little band; my mother, already feeling too visible—already twenty-seven—thought he'd help her. Then, like at the intersection of an X, their paths split and diverged. And she felt betrayed by his success. Not in an obvious, basic way; she just didn't want it.

He didn't mean to do it. Once they were connected in the ether of punk cataloging or whatever, she was ready to go. It had never been about him. I understand this now, after what happened to me. He still didn't get it. Or maybe was in denial.

He thought more work meant somehow becoming better, not greater appeal. This began to be beyond his control. My mother reasoned his ambition got in the way, that she was more legitimate now. But he'd just been doing what he was told, what he thought she wanted. And she'd been waiting for this ticket out all along.

What was he supposed to do? She pushed him there—and then she left. And I was sure she'd leave again. Cementing the one thing she ever really wanted. She had me at twenty-seven, which she always reminded me was why she couldn't have left right away. My father endured and switched places with her—that X again—to be the one who cared for me.

My father talked about this kind of control and tried to convince me to give up the acting or at the very least to do local productions, to write my own stuff. He told me to turn my stories into scripts. Reminding me of all those notebooks, blithely unaware of their incendiary contents. I needed someone to guide me there, an older mentor, someone familiar with that side of things. A Director.

I missed Lucy already. It was 6 p.m., nearly 7, and she'd be in one of her seminars. I realized my mother hadn't called yet to talk about my being expelled, which seemed quite strange. It had been three days. Whenever Josephine texted she would mention my mother and what she was doing, even though I didn't ask. As if she was obscuring the truth of why she'd been absent by charting an itinerary. It didn't really matter to me. What was she going to say? I didn't need to be yelled at.

My father was the gentler one. He'd called immediately and told me he'd come up to see me as soon as he was back in the country. I told him I'd be living twenty minutes away from him in downtown New York by that time. He said he'd be excited to see me. Warned me against taking up with any city men in the meantime. Not even a Director? I flipped over the daybed and sat on it, drawing my backpack next to me.

My phone pinged. A friend of Lucy's had gotten my number from her and texted about a big party at some building on the Lower East Side. Would I like to join? I said yes. Why not? I had nothing to do for a very long time. A few auditions.

I hadn't realized how late it was. I dumped out my backpack and found a pair of jeans and a leather belt-collar necklace with a tortoiseshell buckle. I'd seen a similar one on old pictures of the actress Jacqueline Bisset in my grandmother's magazines. I put both on and searched through the junk on the floor for my tube of musk oil. A little on my neck to mix with the cigarette smoke.

As I was about to leave, the landline rang, which startled, then upset me, reminding me of the call that had come to Lucy's room that day. It took me a moment to register that it was odd the phone had rung at all. Only one person knew the number.

I walked to the wall in the kitchen. "Hello, Josephine." She asked if everything was fine and that I not call her that. I said yes, okay. "Please don't call me on here." She didn't reply as I hung up.

My cell phone shuddered and I looked down at a message from Lucy: "That director is going to be there. The one you met briefly when he came to lecture. Do NOT talk to him. I'm warning you."

I had met him when he came to speak on a panel in Providence. Lucy and I had gone to a screening of his film beforehand. I had watched him from the back row get up and leave after announcing the movie and knew I would see him again. He'd looked at me from the stage during the event as confirmation. And we'd introduced ourselves that evening at a department cocktail.

People had told me his name, but before the lecture I had no idea who he was, what he looked like. I would realize that we had met before, then he had messaged me online and I had deleted it, already feeling the strange negation in his carefully chosen words.

The first thing will signify the last, Josephine sometimes said. Warnings galore. He wound up being in the car with Lucy's friend who came to pick me up.

XV

He turned around and looked at me when I got out of the car and said, "Now I see. It's you again." We all went in to the party and I decided I didn't really care. But I was going to try and follow Lucy's advice. I walked away and poured myself a drink. Pretended I was looking for someone else. An hour later he was at my side. I told him about an author I was interested in, he said he hadn't read him since college. A subtle knock, but a knock nonetheless. He was two decades older than me. I smiled and looked down and someone took a picture of us across the room. He left without saying goodbye.

I saw the image in a text the next day and had to acknowledge that I no longer had no idea. I saw him again at another party later that same week, with an older woman. He acted like he didn't know me. And I cast *him* as the validation I needed. Alone in New York City.

After this first in-person dismissal, I tortured myself that I could have misread someone so badly. He had tried to connect before. This coldness didn't matter, he was simply distracted with other things. Someone should have told me then to stop.

But everyone had. Not just to stop, to not even start. Lucy, again and again. But they didn't know him, either. They only knew of him what was out in the world, I thought, and I knew how wrong that could be.

He came in and out of my life thereafter for weeks. I let him. I would run into him or he would message me, nothing more. Enough to stoke that tiny fire without commitment, not even meeting up. We tried once, but he canceled. It was up to me to do the work and so I did. We ran into each other again. Circumstances intervened: he was already there.

One night he told me he'd deliberately created a life for himself that brought people to him. Moviemaking was like a circuit where people all ended up at the same places. I knew well this old-punk passivity.

I tried to tell him, on the few occasions he asked anything, that we had the same reasons for going into movies. I wasn't in movies yet; but I wanted to be. I thought acting would take me away from dependence on my family. It was certainly not in pursuit of fame or celebrity. It was in spite of them.

I wanted to get jobs all over the place: always new locations and crews.

For him, it was about feeding his needs. Different ones than mine, and yet we were in many ways the same.

Not accountable for connection. Sit back and wait. Not ending or beginning anything. If both are ruled out, possibility—everyone always in play.

Evading commitment is never saying "No."

I knew something wasn't right, so there would be days when I would try to forget him. But he'd sense that. And he wouldn't allow it. If we didn't speak, he wanted to be sure I'd feel him—his absence.

After a few weeks of this—the intermittent hangouts and validation, the guessing—I heard from a third party that he was leaving soon to shoot a new movie, one that had been long in the works, but which he'd never spoken of explicitly. That stung. He was out there, existing on his own. I had latched on to him as my sole thing; most everyone else was still in school. I was only one of his many distractions.

I knew he was off the next day and that he'd been seeing another woman, but he never mentioned her to me—that she existed. That would have implied a commitment to letting me go. He rescheduled our meeting for the daytime, though, no longer the evening. To hurt me, making me think he intended to be clear.

On the bench, he told me he was reading a very difficult Brazilian writer. He pronounced her name incorrectly. I didn't tell him I'd reviewed her work when I had needed to make some money in between shoots. Always, the negation. He crossed his legs away from me. I wondered, why did he keep in touch at all? He paid for my coffee. And then he left and was with her on the trip. And I didn't hear anything until I did.

He was back for a night or two, wanted to have a drink, had read something I suggested. It was always the lede: he was taking a book with him. It bought time. He acted like his interest was real when he wanted attention, and it was my problem when he didn't. It took me so long to realize what he was doing.

And to see that he was most comfortable when there was a barrier between us. Too many negations add up to annihilation. But first, a twisted love story.

He kept inviting me places where there were other people. It was so adolescent, and he was so much older. Grooming me, as he carried the other thing and waited, claiming neither. He took me to the movies, a gesture he would later say meant nothing. And when he finally wanted out, he would tell me that this was the only time he'd felt comfortable with me.

The in-between.

I lost my favorite sweater that night, after we went for a drink, after the movie at the underground piano bar. Gaslighted me. *The sweater was in my closet.*

Then he disappeared again for a few weeks. I always worried I would never hear. If only I'd known that I would, over and over and over. I could have relaxed into the in-between and not wanted it to happen either. Lucy listened patiently to the stories. Over and over and over again. Why did I fight that she was always right. At the start. And in the end.

To have him there, and the promise. That was the only promise he could offer, not a noun but a future tense. If I had understood, I could have manipulated him into forever. But I thought if I showed I was steady and he couldn't rattle me with his inconsistency, maybe he would stay.

He would talk about me to other people, and I would do the same. Exotic, sexy, fascinating. Like I had to audition repeatedly and didn't even know there was no part. *There was never a part.*

I told him this after a time, and he kept his eyes cast downward. I asked him what he wanted, and he said, *that* was the question. He didn't know. He said he didn't want to use me in this way, but the desire was there. Which meant that I was the backup plan, and when I was needed he would let me know. By that point I was too far gone.

I asked him to stop texting me, so he emailed. Told me he wanted to see me and then went silent. He was with her. And then some nights he wanted to come by or to take me to a dinner, but she was there. I didn't understand.

He invited me again to some event. I went. And it was that night, months later, that we finally went to his place. I had Josephine's gold rings on every finger and when I left two were missing.

The night he gave me back the rings he told me to come at a certain time, if I wanted to run into a friend, but I knew she was coming an hour before that. At the end of the night he asked if me and that other woman were still friends, but it sounded like a different question. Like, "Do you still talk to her so she can tell you the truth?" or "Are you two in touch in case I destroy you? I need her for work." Or maybe both.

And it happened again, no longer a one-time thing, and every day or two he would send a message. When I sent one, it felt like I shouldn't, and sometimes he was cruel. We were separated by circumstances, I thought. He never expressed any emotion, except when I pushed and he would placate me or tell me it was okay to be confused, that we would figure it out. And then came more signs that others were there, and I asked, and he said no.

And we sank farther and he would always wait until the very last minute, until I'd wept to Lucy again that he was gone. And he would say he was sorry, that he was over-worked, depressed. I was patient, knowing he'd come back. But as soon as he saw me, he would recognize it all over again. Lucy said, object constancy. I said, what?

That first sensation was really a thirty-fifth, before we ended up back at his place. Each time like he'd forgotten me until he was sure it was the very last moment to show up and remember.

And then, he left on a trip. I didn't know for certain, but it said online that the movie was shooting. And I didn't hear anything until an email saying he had read some-thing I suggested. Same as usual. Buying time. He wanted recognition and response. To give the minimum. These emails came faster when the geographic distance was assured, when he was confident I wouldn't make demands.

How many of us were there? Always something in place to make sure nothing could become real. It was safe there; I didn't understand; hundreds of unfinished stories walk-ing around.

XVI

I couldn't figure out where the noise was coming from at first. I pulled the blanket over my head. It kept clanging, a sound from another time, like a gong. I slowly came to and looked over. The Director was sleeping there, unfazed. He said he liked to sleep at my place because the bed was on the floor. He thought that was very exotic, which is also how he described my parents and grandparents. Bohemian, he would sometimes say with a self-congratulatory smile, smug in his adjacency. It stopped and then started again. I got up, worried that it would wake him. Still ringing. I angrily snatched the receiver off the wall. "Are you kidding me?" I said in an ASMR whisper.

"Margot, your mother is in the hospital."

"Is she okay?" There was silence on the other end of the line. "Josephine!"

"She's in the hospital."

"Northern Westchester?"

"Don't. I mean don't call me Josephine. And don't come. No need. I can handle it, but I wanted you to know." It seemed strange that she would shut this particular bulletin down so fast. Like when she would update me on my mother's schedule, even though I hadn't asked.

"It seems like I should come. I have nothing to do."

"I forbid it."

"Um, okay."

"Why are you whispering like that?"

"No reason."

"Is someone there with you? No one is allowed in the apartment."

"No, but it's the middle of the night. I need to go back to bed."

"Your mother's in the hospital," she scolded.

"You are infuriating. I just said I'd come and you told me not to."

She had already hung up.

XVII

When I woke up that morning, he was gone. On the Thursdays when he stayed over, I would hole up in the old music studio space past the kitchen as he slept. I read scripts in there and practiced lines, sometimes recording a scene and then playing the audio back. At school, I'd bulldozed through all the performance theory straight to more conventional stuff about signs. Whenever I tried to talk to him about this he would pretend to listen, but I knew he felt it wasn't worth his attention. I'd heard he had all kinds of cheap metal statues at his place in L.A.: Oscars, Emmys, things he'd won before me.

He liked me to set the timer to remember to make the coffee for his usual wake-up around 10 a.m. On Thursdays, he had a standing meeting at the New York office of the streaming network where he'd landed some package deal to create content. I would leave him a digest of things I thought were interesting to look at while he drank his coffee. He loved this. The coffee maker was an old metal espresso one from a local cafe that had closed down. It had been my grandfather's favorite place. Josephine had begged the owner to sell her the machine when she heard about the closure.

He liked this detail. The espresso always tasted terrible, metallic. The nozzle so busted that a thin layer of sediment came through in the drip. He didn't care. It was the story, the provenance. A few years back, he'd made a documentary-style movie about jazz of some kind that had included my grandfather's own music and then all the careers he'd helped to make, the records he'd produced.

When he thought I wasn't looking, the Director liked to walk around the place and search out signs of my family. But that morning I got up and he wasn't there. His shoes were gone and he had taken the digest from where I usually left it. No note, only this absence.

I checked my phone and saw I hadn't overslept at all. It was still very early. He never woke up before me. I checked the bathroom and then looked downstairs, looked out the window, but he was nowhere to be seen. I looked at the text messages on my phone, and then the emails, nothing. To be quite sure, I flicked through other apps where he might have left some kind of word. Nothing. But he *had* taken the digest. Was I cast as some kind of secretary, responsible for feeding him ideas and performing favors. I felt it, then. That this was the final time. No more of this over and over.

I knew he wouldn't be back or respond to any messages beyond this point. It wasn't just his disappearance that stung, but that he took my work with him. If he had left the pages, I could imagine him reaching out again as if nothing had happened. He might just . . . never address that morning. Taking the digest meant he would—somewhere, even if he couldn't access it—feel shame, and this would turn into projection. His grandiosity had always been there, hanging above us like one of those thin paper lamps. She had always been there, too.

He couldn't be the one to take me where we would be equals. I would have to do that alone. Maybe then, when everyone else took notice, he might come around. That was the important part about saying nothing. You could come back and fill in the gaps left unsaid. There was no commitment to an ending, no irate commentary logged. So very him. Only emptiness as evidence, a void with every version of the worst.

I ran to the bathroom and threw up the espresso. Get rid of it and then he will show up, holding his empty little cup as usual. I looked in the mirror and wiped my mouth with the back of my hand. I'd texted Lucy a picture of me the day before, and she'd been horrified. I'd lost ten pounds, not on purpose, but because of the way he made me feel, questioning everything. I thought that uneasiness was passion-love.

My appetite was gone all the time, a problem exacerbated by my new habit of chain-smoking out the back window. No one smoked anymore, people always said, but I knew so many who did. He smoked a lot of weed. After I threw up and went to the back window, I saw his ash in the baby-blue porcelain dish. I looked at my phone again. No message. It was nearing ten o'clock. I pushed the ashtray off the sill and watched it smash below.

The landline started to ring.

I had nothing better to do than answer it and, of course, there was the unreasonable thought it could impossibly be him.

It was my grandmother as usual, using the line like a string of tin cans to Westchester. I couldn't tell her what had happened. She would have grilled me on what I'd done to make life so unbearable that he had to go. The Director is what she called him. She still called my grand-father the Jazzman.

Josephine continued talking without a break, announcing that I would have to leave because one of her important friends needed to stay at the apartment. Apparently, the comfort within this relationship was worth more than the comfort of her family. "It's good for you to have to make do, to be uncomfortable. Find a place to go for a week or two." I don't think she imagined that I would never come back. I tried to ask how my mother was doing, if I should visit her, stay with her. But my grandmother wouldn't even broach the discussion.

She told me to go stay with a friend, have some experiences, turn them into good work. I reminded her how she had bristled at the idea of Montana. She said, "No, no, I've changed my mind." Somehow she thought this short-term abandonment would help my art. Her taking away privilege of circumstance was nothing more than yet another performative bid for comeuppance. Of course, no one owed me anything. Still, it was a question of context. Fuck them all.

I would leave.

He wouldn't know where to find me when he didn't come back.

She was still talking but I stopped listening, turned my cell phone around in my left hand, balancing the plastic handset on my shoulder. She went silent, and then that ancient bleat of a cut line. She'd hung up.

I touched my phone and called Lucy. She answered at once. I explained the situation. She told me to book a flight to western Montana, sent me the link even. She said I could stay there indefinitely, and she'd come visit on school breaks. I told her it would only be two weeks, which I believed at the time. As I only had a small amount of stuff, I could pick up and go at any moment. She said to leave the next day. I didn't argue.

Still feeling nauseous, I pulled my backpack out of the cupboard. Dropped it on the floor and ran to the guest bathroom, while fastening my hair with the elastic that had been around my wrist. I threw up again, but this time dry. Lifting myself up to look into the mirror over the sink, I saw a small drop of blood coming from my nose. I had only felt my gut turn over. No bile, but blood from the violence of the heaving. I used the back of my hand to wipe it off my face and onto the mirror. Then I slammed the door behind me. Camille would clean it and never mention it to Josephine. Her job had always been to tidy up what happened at the city apartment when my grandfather stayed there. So Josephine wouldn't have to know. To acknowledge.

I was angry that she had thought it fine to throw me out, reasoned it away as thoughtful necessity. Almost laughable, all her distortions and denials. I opened the linen closet and tossed the folded layers onto the floor. Behind them was the metal box. I knew it was there because I had seen it when her friend, the cleaner, had been called to open it and take her weekly wages. She thought I wasn't looking, but I watched the whole thing. Of course, Josephine would never use Venmo or any kind of electronic system. She stored ready cash in the linen closet, in a lockbox with a few rare cassette tapes and some jewelry. I knew the code because it was the same one she used for the alarm at the Westchester house—my grandfather's birthday: 01/11/1932.

I took about $2,000, a huge emerald ring, and a gold choker that had a white paper tag tied on with thread, hand-labeled "Alice Coltrane." It was hard to decipher. I felt so weak that I couldn't be bothered packing. Two pairs of jeans, a t-shirt, black lace underwear, and a silk blouse the Director had bought me for auditions were stuffed into my backpack. I put the money in the front part and decided to wear the necklace. I ended up in an old black shirt, corduroy pants, baby blue indoor soccer shoes, and a golden choker. It came from India as far as I could tell. There was a red stone in the middle of the medallion shield at the center and two strands of chain ran from there to the two diamond shapes at either side. Tiny flickering gold bars hung all around the lower edge. I took one of the baseball caps off of the hook by the door and put it on, adjusted it in the hall mirror and added the sunglasses, then shouldered the backpack. I noticed the Director had left bits of moss or dirt on the floor. His fingerprints were also on the front door. I could tell because his hands were always greasy with some kind of salve.

XVIII

"Margot Highsmith?"

I'd meant to call Lucy on the ride to her parents' house, but I stayed glued to the window, looking. It had been so long since I'd been this far away from a city. This was different than Providence, or Josephine's. There were no houses for miles. I tried talking to the driver, but she, like my recent seatmate, wanted nothing to do with me. There were moments when I caught her in the rearview mirror staring at my necklace. Or maybe she was looking at the inflamed demilune above. Either way, she was repelled by how ostentatious or debased I was, sitting there in her backseat. As if all of it was communicable through the space of the car. I was the city descending, with my clothes, systems, ideas. She didn't want to chat. But when she did speak it was as if she'd been holding it inside for too long. The words exploded out with an accent I couldn't identify.

"Weyeeeere almost theyere."

"Really? That was fast."

"Nothing is very far." I nodded in reply and my phone fell down the back crack of the seat. I looked away from her stare and used my left hand to dig behind the plastic cover. A few circles of stale cereal came out with it. "You lose something?"

"I found it, thank you."

"Can you not eat in the car, please."

"I—" I started to speak and then stopped. It didn't matter. I scooped up the cereal and unzipped the front of the backpack and put it there for safekeeping. Then I pressed my face to the window to see what almost there looked like. There were fields of arid yellow grass, wooden sticks along the perimeters. In the distance, mountains, rolling in fading curves behind greenery, a tree, three, some pines. Two horse trailers alone in a field. The curtains on their windows printed with cartoon turtles. I could see this from the road only because they were parked as if about to turn and join the highway. Durston Road. Jackrabbit Lane. A strip mall. Were those cows? Or bison? Different cows than those counted by Josephine, anyway. The trees larger and more numerous the further we went from the airport. Big sky. High rocks, a shallow river. Repeat. Someone standing in the current, water to his waist, windmilling his arms. The trees became denser and bore needles rather than leaves, growing to points. There were empty chairlifts swinging back and forth ahead of the stoplight, suspended from tightrope high wires. I was auditioning for everyone here now. Already putting it on for the driver.

A huge rusty maple tree loomed larger as we neared the turn. The road there was slick with orange leaves. I felt the car slide as she tried to brake. Left onto Plinth Road.

No houses for a few minutes, and then one mailbox at the end of a very long driveway. And then another, this one with chalked white letters: "Neher." Or maybe the N was a W. The H was a Y. Two more mailboxes, and finally the one marked "57 Plinth Road," written by hand in black marker on a ribbed aluminum sheet. I suddenly thought about the Director: he was fifty-seven.

For a moment, for some reason, I thought about what it would be like to call my mother and talk this all through with her. Lucy did that. And I did that with Lucy's mother sometimes, but never with Rose. Now Josephine had said she wasn't well and that I shouldn't think about her. And suddenly she needed me to get out of where I should have been welcome. And he'd left. So I'd left, too. Went to Montana.

The woman was driving very carefully over the rough path leading to Lucy's. "This is some house," she said.

"Not mine." This intrigued her, or made her more suspicious.

"This the right address?"

"Yep." She pulled the van as close as she could without hitting the wall. And laughed a little to herself. I pushed the brown button to open the door and pulled the plastic handle to the right. She kept on grinning, watching out the front window. I pulled my backpack up from the seat next to me and hopped onto the wet ground. There was no paving, only cobblestones worn down in formation.

"You sure you're not breaking in here?" she called out after rolling down her window. The house was dark and untouched.

I shook my head and waved goodbye from the side porch, where I'd climbed the wooden steps. Her window went up. She needed to gaze away before I could locate the key in the secret spot that Lucy told me. It was funny how we both saw each other as a threat. The longer I idled before going inside, the more she would think I wasn't supposed to be there. If I went ahead and got the key, she would know its whereabouts. Suspended in refusal. A pause, playing chicken.

She rolled down the window again, and before she could speak I said, "I forgot I had to collect the mail," and headed down the driveway. And then, to win, she backed up past me. I felt like I should take a photo of her license plate or at least remember it. Fifty-seven and these kinds of things: 1ZX890. As soon as the car was out of sight, I turned and headed back up to the house. I left my backpack by the rose bushes, flipped over the wrong rock, then started towards the flower beds to find the key.

I lifted another flat stone. With nothing underneath but two entwined pill bugs, all silver overlaps like the CD player from that time long ago, a kind of childish joy to them. I covered them up, careful they wouldn't be suffocated. Beneath the next stone I saw the corner of a thick wooden slat. I bent down and dusted the soil from the top. The rectangle grew larger, and dirt compacted under my fingernails. It lifted out easily. Pressed into the earth were two keys on a metal circle. I slid it around my wrist and walked back to the roses to get my bag.

I stopped in front of the third rose bush, its tiny pink blooms. They looked like climbing roses, but they had nothing to hold on to. A faint shape in the dirt, as if a tent had once been there. Four stake holes, just far enough away in the earth. Two were lit up, the others in shadow. Nightfall; still dressed in the clothes from the plane, my shirt collar hardened dry. I carried the backpack with my left hand, the key in my right and walked slowly towards the front door. It suddenly occurred to me that I might not be able to work the lock. The door looked heavy and ancient, steel. Like the one in my father's studio.

I should have warned my father to be careful what he asked for. That, yes, something—someone—new would monopolize my mind. This story. No more trailers, no more early call times, no more alternative realities as openings for abuse and isolation.

XIX

On days like that, I had to shower to feel dry. It was always damp there. I learned this quickly. My first week was spent in bed, listening. I collapsed as soon as I got inside. Had no appetite, no energy, and I'm not sure which came first or caused the other.

There were moments when I thought about getting up and walking to town, and at these times I also imagined running into the minivan driver again. Or getting her if I called a car on my phone. For some reason she haunted me, however awkwardly, like the four deep holes in the front yard. One morning I made what felt like a genuine effort to get up and explore the grounds, but after a moment's distraction I found myself back in the fetal position on the master bedroom floor, the source of the feeling unclear. What was the loss?

Attending my own graduation? I didn't give a fuck. Some asshole. Yes. That was it. And it wasn't even him, not really, but the absence of a narrative for what had happened. All this speculation, a sad little cliffhanger. My daydreams ran from good to bad to good again. He would be back. Wait, no, it was over. Done. Gone. *Arrivederci*, Director. But then again, who knows! And around again we go. It felt pathetic to be so upset, to dare claim that at some point there had been some kind of disconnect, a denial, one that led to the inevitable. I was aware that when I told myself the story, whatever flavor of it I fancied that day, it was never me at fault. And I knew there was a lot wrong with me. Lots! But I also knew that he had gamed it so I had no agency. And I believed what his actions showed me about myself. This is the dangerous thing about a breakup with someone so much older and so much more accomplished when you are young, desirous of credibility and short on self-love: when he goes, he rips those little medals right off your chest and carries them away with him.

One might advance the case of my parents as a counter-argument and point out that, once the media clocked them together, the benefits of joint cachet lasted forever; the association ran on beyond their relationship's full stop. As if that credibility was always there. The reality was a little different. Another kind of cognitive dissonance. And I saw it hurting my mother when she wasn't looking. She wanted to control *everything*. Lucy once explained that the opposite of love—vulnerable love—was control. And my whole family was obsessed with control. While simultaneously harping on about resistance to state or corporate interference, and slipping that control. So confusing, always.

I didn't care about eating, only sleeping and not thinking. Josephine called every day at the same time, saying she was worried about me. I assured her I was fine and asked after my mother. Her response was always the same dismissive sound. My father emailed, still ending every note with the signature of his first name. Josephine texted so often that she had stopped signing off. I responded to maybe one in seven.

Lucy called every day at 3 p.m., after her seminar. I didn't say much, afraid to *ressasser* and push her away. She said some people can mirror or magnify others without being in pursuit of connection—it's actually easier. And asked every other call if I'd explored the grounds yet. And I would say "No," not mentioning that I had barely left the bedroom. The entire floor was covered in brown carpet, which I preferred to the bed. After six days, I decided to take the key out of the pale blue ceramic ashtray where I'd left it by the front door.

I had heard the rain arrive the night before. Blood caught in a tin cup. Lucy's house was designed by one of those architects who knew how to bring the outside in. City people think they want to try and keep it out, but once they leave the city they want even the weather to come in. This admission was enough to stir me from my carpet and lead me to the lawn. I sat on my hands during the storm to stop them flailing and to keep a little more of me tethered. When my head felt like it was lifting away and I was soaked through to my marrow, I got up and went hunting for something to eat.

There was nothing left from my last shop. I had left the house once, to find my way to town. Lucy had become concerned about my eating after I sent her another photo of myself in the bathroom mirror. She made me promise to cycle into town and buy fresh food. She had drawn a map, taken a picture, and texted it to me. Then told me where to find the bike in the back. There was a tiny shed next to the big one, which I still hadn't dared investigate. I wanted to save that a bit longer, to have something to look forward to. I was beginning to feel numb, something I hadn't experienced in a long while.

I had texted Josephine that I was going to take time off phone calls and any sort of communication with her. She agreed right away, which threw me a little. Wasn't she always watching? Or else she was hiding something. She had taken it too easily. Nothing was ever accepted that limited her control. But when I asked about my mother, Josephine was quick to end the call. Something kept me from calling her myself, knowing that it would ignite things I didn't want to touch just then. Instead, I rehashed the Director's departure over and over. Lucy put up with it. I felt the strain on her, though.

So, I tried to speak to no one for that week and then some. To see if I could do it, to spare Lucy. But a part of me remained stuck on that last night on the floor, on that floor in New York. I constantly wanted to check up on the Director, to see who he was with, where he was. This kind of masochism was what I imagined cutting had been like for Lucy: both banal and irresistible. She told me about it when I first saw her arms during our freshman year. I'd tried it myself when I was in high school, and felt, drum roll, nothing. I told her so and she shrugged.

"Stop the *ressasse*," Lucy would text me daily, knowing where I would go without her. She had prescribed me these weeks at her house and I was trying to behave—to eat a bit, and behave. My standard evening meal was a frozen chocolate bar. I would put it in a plastic bag and smash it on the counter. I struggled to sleep on an empty stomach, so for the second course I would take three Benadryl from my mother's jeweled case. Sometimes simply swallow them. On very bad days, grind them with the bottom of a can, my makeshift pestle. Then put them in the plastic bag, shaking it up so that the hot pink dust stuck to the white nougat.

For no clear reason, I reached for my phone that Tuesday night and touched the word "Rose." It went straight to voicemail, which never happened. Oddly for someone so set on being detached and aloof, my mother always answered the phone. That incongruous "profession-alism." It had been longer than ever since we'd spoken. Josephine had told me not to bother her. I imagined Josephine hiding her phone, first in the hospital and then at home, taking it away somehow. No matter that she was a grown woman with a child of her own. This was Josephine's way. I had felt relieved not to have to deal, to tell her she may have been right about my pursuit of drama.

XX

No one had stayed at the house in years or bothered to check on its dilapidation. Lucy's mother had a thing against Airbnb. The handrail on the left of the landing was coming away, red paint scaling off like a bloody fishtail. I could see it vibrating loosely at the top whenever I held the other end below. The staircase was so wide and hollow that if someone were filming a scene head-on, they could see straight through. Two people passing, one up, one down. And the metal spiral, once red too, painted black.

It was all very beautiful, by some architect whose name I couldn't pronounce back when I was able to remember it. There had once been another house on the property, where Lucy's grandparents had lived. It was uncommon in that part of Montana to have that kind of space. The rest of the houses, the little I could see of them from the road, seemed to be more conventional and alike. It was only Lucy's that looked like this, half made of glass, way up there. Metal in places it usually didn't go and wood, wood everywhere. Some parts painted, others once polished, now dull and dirty. There were two small guest houses out back. One was where Lucy's father had gone when he needed to work on deadline for some book project or article. The Director had worshipped him. So much so that he took noticeably more interest in me after I mentioned Lucy. I should have told him it was her who issued warning number one.

When Lucy's father died, there were countless tributes to him and a big obituary in the *Times*. He had become something more than a critic, people said; positively a prophet, according to the more hysterical tributes. He foretold all the mini screens we'd have, but then so did so many others. His more theoretical works were soaked in that stuff after he came back from a spell in France. Dusty old works from the '70s, a grail for people like the Director.

Lucy's grandfather had come from a line of industrialists, that's what Lucy said, without specifying, and refused to say more. So they had big weird houses in many different places, like this one—but also, probably, nothing like it at all. We didn't discuss the other homes. Montana was her favorite, and it had been her father's, too. I understood after being there how easy, how useful it was to become strange to oneself. Alone in a room in the woods for days on end. No regularly scheduled distractions or prompts, the opposite of a set life, but a set life all the same.

This house was the elder statesman of the town, surveying everything else. The "57" an artifact from its first life, a way to name the land, this house was more beast than street number. That was the only thing that made the few interactions I had with people in town make sense. They were suspicious of my privilege.

Mistrustful of my showing up by choice, just to stay indoors. My first week there I couldn't bring myself to open a door or even a cupboard. Self-pitying and pathetic, my curiosity restrained by fear and sadness.

Lucy had told me to help myself to anything in the house, that it was stocked with blankets, food. One could survive there during a hypothetical apocalypse for months on end. After six days on the floor, I upgraded to the mattress in the main bedroom. Someone had left a top sheet on it and a lonely pillow at the headboard. I took the sheet off and left it bare, with its depressed bulb-shapes stitched over blue satin fabric stained with brown rings. I didn't turn any handle or knob, and only entered the rooms that were already open: front door up the stairs to the bedroom to hall and back. I existed above the house for days.

I lived on the bars I'd thrown into my backpack when I stopped at the gas station and the candy I bought at the store when I started taking daily bike rides. Sometimes I shared the nuts with the birds at the cemetery. My backpack stayed in the middle of the floor, flung open. I had left the Coltrane necklace—that was how I thought of it—hanging from the hook next to the sink by the bath. The laundry room was somewhere downstairs. It could also be reached by a door accessible through a hatch in its ceiling. This made it easy for me to drop my things through and take care of them later. There were closets full of t-shirts, worn sweaters and a few old, waxed coats. And Lucy had been right, there were enough blankets and assorted supplies to last a cold, lonely winter.

I had found the bicycle in the tiny shed, as Lucy had instructed. And then I discovered the large freezer she'd mentioned. She had joked about once finding a boa curled up in there. The image had stayed with me and made me a little fearful to go on the hunt for frozen chicken nuggets or waffles. Some mornings I worried about what would happen if I consumed 5,000 percent of a week's Vitamin A, clocked entirely from all those nutrition bars. These frets passed whenever a text buzzed in that reminded me why I had no appetite. I know it's painful, Lucy wrote over and over, her boilerplate back-pats.

All the same, I wasn't ready to do anything at all but zombie my way through the days. I'd play both game show host and contestant to keep myself amused. *What's behind painted door number eight?* Each day, I'd be allowed to crack open a cabinet. A lottery to occupy the what's next. It went on for three weeks. The three weeks and three days before I met Graves.

XXI

Later that afternoon, the Shop Man followed me out of the store and watched me from the shadow of the awning. I put the jeweled case in the wire basket of the red bike I'd found on my arrival three weeks earlier. I had put down a bandana to keep my purchases from falling through. I was very pleased with this construction and reckoned it would work fine so long as I kept an eye on the knots tying it to the basket. The Shop Man was still watching as I tightened the edges once more. The cigarette case, vegetables, seeds, and candy all looked snug and secure. A cigarette had materialized in his left hand, and he took a slow drag and glared. I nodded at him and bent down to tie the yellow barrel laces of my boots. They were always coming undone. I had found a few pairs of these gummy-soled shoes in the back of Lucy's closet. They were a little too big, but they were fine if you crisscrossed the laces through the metal tabs tightly enough.

It wasn't far from the center of town to the highway that led to Plinth Road. I heard my father's music in the back of my head as I made the turn from the sidewalk onto the street: lyrics rather than music, maybe. Him singing, yelling, singing-yelling, whatever you called it when someone made a sound like that. It wasn't shouting—that was what he did with my mother towards the end. A sing-yell, so different. Josephine did neither. Lucy told me once that her father never spoke, only shouted.

Whenever I made that turn on my bike, I heard my father's voice, like the playback from a voicemail. This led me to imagine my mother's leave-a-message too. "She's checked out. You know how it goes," Josephine said whenever I asked. Or she ignored the question. That day it came louder than usual and I turned my head for a second, half wondering if she was there. The silence and Josephine's reticence like a hoax in aid of a surprise. My mother would make good after all these years on her promise to come.

Her voice again instead of his, singing. I looked back towards the road and hugged the curve on the street as the path gave way to the fast lane. Five racing bikes were ahead of me, neon-clad riders in formation. I glided a little and then pushed up so that I was standing without touching the seat. A pick-up truck came swerving around the little bend, fast, edging into my lane and out again and sending a shower of tiny meteorites up, missing my eyes but peppering the front of me. I felt nothing but saw them bounce away. It was all so fast, just a flash and then the frame of my bike sliding out under me. Somehow, I caught myself and was able to regain control before I crossed the white line into doom traffic. The exit to the graveyard was on the right and I felt myself taking it, knowing that something was off with me but unsure of much else. I swatted my face and coughed as heavy, metallic-scented dust blew up.

I hadn't intended to go by the cemetery that day; the plan had been to get back to the house with my supplies and settle in again. It was Friday, not Tuesday. Tuesday afternoon was when I would go to feed the birds among the headstones. One near collision had my schedule all askew. Friday meant hours spent staring at the laptop screen waiting for a message to show up, a polite alert that might shift a gear for me. I still half-hoped for a note from my agent, though I'd asked her not to write, saying I needed time to collect what was left of myself. Still, she had replied quickly, agreeing that I should take this time to work on some writing projects or finding a book I might want to adapt. I had laughed as I deleted it. Even so, I couldn't help hoping she would disregard my request and send something dramatic and life-altering to lure me back into the world. Wherever I was, it was not the World. But I was open to the notion of a major shift. And, yes, I hoped it would bring me in front of the Director.

On Fridays in this not-World there were crows, other days I'd seen blue jays and starlings. Only crows at the turn, like the murder, I remembered. They used to sit at the foot of the vines that climbed the back wall. Both the ivy and the bricks placed there by Josephine's landscape architect were supposed to look like they'd found their way on their own. I felt a little like that out there, wanting to seem like Montana suited me.

The northwestern crows seemed bigger, their wingspan larger, end tail feathers trailing on the ground. I noticed this the first time I saw one, sweeping the dirt as it walked side to side. The one closest to the road flew up at me, nearly hitting my handlebars. I could see the luminescent green on its back, spiny little feet held in as it maneuvered over, beady eyes staring down.

My path to the gate was automatic: left, left, then right. I felt like I was riding out that last stretch as on a wave, the wheels floating over the gravel, until that crow almost hit me in the face. The gate, which was always left ajar, was closed. I put my feet down with the bicycle balanced between my legs and something in my stance felt wrong, like one leg had grown suddenly and left me with a compensating lean.

A man was waving at me from beyond the gate.

He came slowly into focus. I fixed him with a squint as he grew larger and larger. He was full-size now, up good and close; six feet and a half cut into bars—slices—by the iron poles of the gate. I was bewildered and shook my head. We locked eyes again and he opened his mouth. I felt dizzy, and squeezed my eyelids together. He said, "Look down," his voice descending to a growl.

"I'm sorry, what?"

"Do you need help?" His hair seemed like it hadn't been cut in months. It was curly and dark brown. He had a distinct chin and black eyes. They looked sleepy, permanently so. "You're bleeding." I closed my eyes: the kaleidoscope seat. Red, blue, iridescent hash. Grass.

"I think it's fine," I said.

"It's not fine." He kept speaking with that strange calm.

"I don't feel much of anything."

"You need to go to the hospital. There's something lodged in there." He bent over. "Hold on." He took a key from his pocket and unlocked the gate, shaking it three times before it yielded and he stepped backward. He looked me first in the eyes (to signal attraction, hello?) before kneeling to examine the wound. That was the first time I mistook his interest for intrigue.

"Look, let's just grab your bike and get in my truck. I can take you."

I returned his look and laughed: "Who are you?"

"We can get into that later."

"I should get in a truck with the man who has the cemetery key?"

"You're losing blood. We don't have time to argue." It was an epic seduction. He was already telling me what to do.

I had never seen this man before, this man who was already so familiar, already so dismissive. He was big enough that I'd have noticed and handsome enough that I'd have remembered, but perhaps not in a way that everyone would like. We were staring at each other as if we were both remembering an old story: half amusement, half disbelief, blood pooling at our feet, trickling towards the cemetery. I knew it wasn't wise to go with him, but my feelings had been running contrary to wisdom.

"You don't feel anything at all?" he asked, looking down at my leg again. I could see some small pebbles in the exposed flesh. Below the wound a thick red stripe ran down my shin and into my boot. "I was a trauma surgeon once upon a time." I decided I would believe this on account of his steadiness—that pathological calm. "May I?" he asked, before touching my skin. He took off the long-sleeve shirt he was wearing. I watched him pull it over his head, a flash of his own skin. Then he pulled down the stained t-shirt underneath, wrapping the other one as a tourniquet around my leg.

I put my arm around his shoulders and let the bike fall beside him, the wheel tracking blood as it spun around. He lifted me up under my legs. We went to the side of his truck parked in the dirt by the gate. He opened the door and eased me in, placing the bloody leg on the dashboard. Still feeling nothing, I turned to look through the back window. There were assorted shovels, some mulch, and long wooden boards. A *serial killer*, I thought. Trauma surgeon, right. Whatever. It would be more exciting than the Benadryl.

"I really don't feel anything."

"You could be in shock," he said.

"No, this has happened before."

He looked up, startled. "What do you mean?" I didn't know how to explain it. The stain on the pink moiré of my pinafore on tour; the satin shoes; all the hangnails and endless bandages; the burns; the bruise below my bottom lip.

"It's hard to explain."

"What are you doing here?" As if he no longer needed an answer to his first question.

"In your truck? I have no fucking idea."

He had climbed into the driver's seat and started off on the road to the local ER. "No, I mean in this god-awful town."

"What are *you* doing here? Why would a trauma surg—"

"I don't practice medicine anymore. I came here to think, got here last week."

"Me too. Well, a few weeks ago." We sat in silence. I realized he was the first person I'd spoken to at any length aloud.

"What were you doing at the cemetery?" I asked, but we were already pulling up at the hospital and he ignored me—now giving that same sure wave to an attendant.

"I'm sorry, I can't stay with you. Something I have to take care of, but take my number and let me know how it goes. Give me your phone."

"Just tell me your number." His need for control was lovely and clear, as was his delight in this burst of adrenaline I'd brought about. "Give it to me," he repeated. I handed it to him. He typed something in.

The tourniquet was solid red. I grabbed the phone back and pressed Call. His ringer must have been off.

"New York?" I asked.

"Yes."

"Me too, kind of." I tried to figure out his age; he looked too young to have years and years of surgery school behind him. Maybe he was full of shit.

"She needs a wheelchair," he called out to the woman attending. This was a bare-bones operation. Only in such a small town could you yell out the window of a pickup truck like that. Sensing my uneasiness, he laughed. Two hospital aides were coming towards my side of the vehicle. He turned off the engine and got out to come around and lift me gently into the chair before they had a chance to. "What do I do with her bike?"

"Hold onto it for her," the aide said. "We have no storage here."

He looked at me with expectant dark eyes.

"It's not so bad," the other woman said, with a tight smile that suggested otherwise.

"Later," he said, and lifted his chin as he climbed back into the truck.

I saved his number as "Graves."

XXII

He must have twenty years on me, I decided, coasting on his calm and fine lines both.

A trauma surgeon. What does it take to push someone that way? You don't avoid the most unexpected tragedies; you invite them. What is there to fear. You know you will see the worst. You have control. Resurrecting lives. Setting up stories. Dealing with pain.

I was free-associating, disassociating, going in and out from some "pain medication" the first attending doctor had given me. My body felt the same, the high behind my eyes. All red to black to colors that slowed down once I opened them. And then the images became fast, faster. My mother pale, blue skin, denim on denim. Him, Graves— whatever his name was—pixelated. Then rapidly growing larger and larger through gate-jail bars. The man at the checkout. Nuts. Candies. Tender exchange.

And sounds came, but played backwards, mismatched. My mother's voice singing, screaming. My father shouting. Josephine divining. Graves again. The Director. Lucy. A warning. The town encouraging me with eyes and nods. A hand beckoning. "Go ahead." And then, in a whisper, "You won't make it through if you do." A tour bus. Parking lot after parking lot. "You won't find what you are looking for." That infinity loop always there: the thing that will keep you going until it collapses, because you touched it. Real means it's over; you got close enough.

The nurse came back and checked the dressing on my leg. She said something about me being lucky. They had done seven stitches, could have been twenty. Debris had flown up from the road. Pushed its way deep under my skin.

That was what the other man and his assistant had been digging around for. Heads bobbing, two metal tools between them. Unspoken agreement. Metal to flesh. Out again to gloved hand and then placed on the tray.

The nurse telling me that the bits of grit could have caused an epic infection. They kept asking if it hurt while they dug. And I kept saying no.

"Does that hurt, on a scale of—"

"No," I said again.

But the doctor wouldn't stop hassling, asking about pain levels. One of my father's songs came up in the background muzak. I groaned. "On a scale—?"

"Zero. I just hate this song." He glanced at his assistant. I watched him take the slender caliper and jab it into my leg. He looked up at me, embarrassed, when he felt my eyes on him. It was the wrong thing to do. Hippocratic oath. But it caused no reaction. And neither of us wanted to discuss it further.

XXIII

The hospital aide called a town taxi when I was discharged. I hadn't been able to see clearly on my phone. I hit the screen three useless times, only to drop the thing on the floor. She didn't bend to pick it up, just stared at me like I was a sideshow freak. While I was angling myself downward to reach it, another nurse walked by and tutted at me to stand straight. She bent down and picked up the phone, delivering it to my right hand. The other woman pretended she'd been paged elsewhere. I was left alone, watching the cars pull up around me, picking up and dropping off those that needed care.

A black sedan with a stick-on Taxi label stopped in front of me. The other nurse reappeared, apologizing for having thrown out Graves's shirt. It had been a lucky plaid tourniquet. As she said this she looked at me as if bracing herself to be attacked. I was making strange impressions on the people of Montana. I didn't react to her tension. She opened the car door and I climbed in, eyes flashing up at her. She slammed it shut. I indulged a cruel notion and waved at her through the back window. She stood there staring.

"Where are we going?" the driver asked as we moved off. For a split second I imagined he was the suspicious woman from the airport commute. His features shifting, cheekbones higher, lips thicker, beard gone. Then I saw him as he was: neck craned back, hooded eyes, fierce teeth. I was confused again. "I asked for the address," he said nastily. I was so used to summoning vehicles on apps that I'd forgotten this interaction was a thing.

"Oh, sorry: fifty-seven Plinth Road."

"You live in that big house?"

"I am staying there."

"I've never been down that road. There was a tree that fell—"

"It's clear now. I rode my bike that way."

"Not anymore," he said, squinting over his shoulder and flicking his chin at my bandaged leg. I didn't respond. When he faced the road again, we locked eyes in the rearview mirror. I looked away, slumped lower in the seat to watch the trees through the window, smaller as we drove on.

The driver didn't need to ask for directions or if we'd arrived at the right place. There was only one house it could be. He growled as he rolled up the driveway. Then checked for my gaze, recognition. I gave him no such satisfaction, just an extra $10 as a thank you for not talking and never coming back. He understood and didn't offer to help me out of the car. I fumbled and just managed to make it, hobbling to the front door. And he pulled away, looking back only through the rearview mirror.

XXIV

The bandage on my leg was turning a shade of off-white that matched the walls in Lucy's living room. In the middle of the space was a pit entirely upholstered in a soft citrus fabric, swimming-pool style. A conversation pit, they called it. Rectangular, almost square, deep enough to make it tricky to climb in and out. Velvet cushions all around, orange like drugstore soda. The colors showed up lovely in the evening, when the late sun dipped to the right angle. All those big windows letting everything in, light slanted towards the center. A fire pit.

I sat there in the middle where the beam hit my phone. Big views on all sides. The one to the north leading out to a mountain top, a soft shadowy bend in the sky. In the background, the tallest pine in the woods made them all a sharp pyramid. To the right and left, rows of skinny-trunked white trees.

It might have been harder to climb out had I been appropriately aware, and appropriately concerned, about my leg, but if I didn't think about it consciously there was no sensation to remind me. So whenever I needed the bathroom or fancied a snack, I'd pull up on my arms and swing my right leg up and over. There were steps on the other side, but I preferred it this way, to roll myself over onto the plush floor. Every flat surface here was carpeted. I was forever comparing it to my father's place, the difference was so striking: concrete floors in contrast to wall-to-wall pile. The perfect place to *ressasser* all day. Despite its neuroticism there was a lazy quality to the word. Lucy knew. I went to text her but then, on impulse, dialed my mother's number instead. Straight to voicemail.

Simpler to just stay there all day and watch my phone. My leg felt fine, but the stern way the doctor had said to not put weight on it had frightened me. So I decided to sleep downstairs in the guest room, with its austere '80s decor and big king-size bed on a stacked plastic frame. The floor carpeted in the same blankness, a dusty, matte white. The only light came from one monstrous hunchback lamp, its spine curling over into a funnel shade.

I missed the mattress upstairs, it reminded me of sleeping on the floor in New York and then of other things. This strange modular pit made Montana feel farther away. A house like a movie set.

Some mornings when I woke up downstairs, I thought about pretending to be an icy character, cruel even, to play a new role for the day. This was a fine set for an '80s period piece, and if I stepped into the right character, I wouldn't miss anyone. Not the Director, not Lucy. Even the bathroom was tiled Memphis Group turquoise and wallpapered black-and-white like TV static. All helpful to detach from city realities and the natural world outside. Nothing warm, wet, or emotional. The living room, with its deep soft recess, felt like the only space susceptible to melodrama.

I thought about how my father once told me that he found coolness as an old man. The story I'd always heard was that he'd lost it. No, he said, cool came to him when he decided to no longer go after things. He set it up so that everyone would have to find him. And they did. He went full detachment. I think my mother caused this desire of his to withhold. He gave her more effort than he'd ever given anything, but that didn't make her stay.

He changed himself when it was already too late to become what he thought the person who abandoned him wanted. So much character development happens this way. Self-cancellation. Don't love me. You'll get no results.

Works every time.

But then my mother couldn't go back. There were always people around, women. My father didn't seem to care, really, wanted only what was unavailable. They all—especially the women—wanted proximity to whatever it was he had. He only needed to show up. Old-punk passive.

When I was sixteen, that time when my mother came home for a while, she told me one night, high on pills, that she sometimes wanted to go back. Go back where? I asked. And she just shook her head. That auburn hair swept from side to side, like the ride at the amusement park where the chairs fling outward, remaining equidistant as they revolve. Her hair was like mine, so thick she could hide behind it with only the tops of her ears showing. A tall elf-creature, always in denim and boots.

I felt the loneliness I knew she hid from me by touring, being busy, producing. She was always pretending to value the collective, but she kept on working hard to generate ever more work for herself. It made for a confused lesson in collectivism. Her work never would, never could run out.

I felt uneasy when I thought about how long it had been since we spoke.

I put my phone in my back pocket before I scaled the side of the couch to get a snack. But then, feeling intensely bothered by its weight all of a sudden, I pulled it out and threw it into the middle of the pit where it landed face down—perfect, now it couldn't look at me for a while. I had turned the ringer off weeks ago, as if that would make the call I was waiting for come, and come in louder.

XXV

I managed to lever myself back into the pit, tossing some packets of peanuts in before me for sustenance. Flipping the phone over, I saw that grey-green box. I wanted the missed call to be one of two people.

It was neither.

Strangely, the caller was trying again.

Graves.

"Hello?"

"It's—" His voice broke up. He hadn't told me his real name. "I wanted to know how you were doing. Where are you?"

"I'm trying to rest my leg, laying low."

"How are you feeling?"

"I feel fine. The same."

"Right." There was a long pause on the end of the line. I thought he might hang up. "I have some supplies to drop off."

"Supplies?"

"Things to dress the wound, stuff you won't find easily here." I wanted to say that I could just go to the store. What would I possibly need that I couldn't find there. The store had range. His directives made me uneasy, reverse-charmed by that same calmness. First it had been his eyes, and then that voice. Its tone projected gentleness, but somehow I felt threatened. "Let me drop some things by. There's something I want to tell you." I heard him breathe in sharply. A last plea: "I have your bicycle."

Manners, Josephine would say. Don't seem ungrateful.

He'd saved me in the cemetery.

"It's fifty-seven Plinth Road."

"See you soon."

XXVI

I didn't know what direction he was coming from. It didn't much matter, there was nothing I could do in such a short time. I'd used a few dishes in the kitchen when I'd tried to feel civilized, eating a nutrition bar with fork and knife or counting out gummy bears. They were all in the sink still, residue hard. Empty water bottles were poking out of the garbage bag rigged beside the metal trash can. The only thing I could smell was the musk I'd brought with me, though the circling flies signaled something else. I never thought anyone would come over. The Director had been the only person I'd allowed into the city apartment. I knew it would impress him, and this factor outweighed everything else. To be validated then discarded and validated again and discarded. Until I left. After he left. And now, the gameshow at Lucy's house. I left the living room and hopped over to Door #1 to see if I could find any alcohol to offer my guest. He still hadn't offered his name. Behind the first metal door, there were some linens and shelves of electric-yellow glasses, colored but clear. Lucy called it "Vaseline glass." She'd told me about her mother's collection, made during the years when radioactive uranium was part of the melted composition. It glowed in the closet under the ultraviolet light.

Behind Door #2 was a wet bar with a lock. I realized I had left the key ring in the basket of my bicycle—such opportune timing, Mr. Graves. Maybe there was alcohol in the back shed? I hated going out there. Everything smelled like damp grass. This reminded me of my mother. She always looked wet, either her hair or under her eyes. I closed the door and shut my eyes hard to shake off the thought. I wanted to call her again. Josephine wasn't my guardian. My mother was. Fuck Josephine. Everyone I was supposed to love had ceded control to her, even my father, in strange ways. As I backed out of the kitchen, I noticed a faded sheet of paper covered with codes and passwords in black ink attached to the fridge door by small tears of yellow artist's tape. The doorbell rang, a strange noise; dampness had set into the bell too.

There were a thousand ways I could rationalize my bad decision. I didn't even know if it was bad, just that it *might* be. But he had saved my life, pretty much. And that was the opposite of bad. For some people. Should I call my mother again before answering the door? She hated to text. I had to try one more time. He had called again after I didn't pick up. It takes a certain kind of person to do this. Missed calls log. My mother had not called back. Again, the bell! He had no limits. Should I not answer? Would she answer? His call had thrown me. He was already here.

I went into the bathroom to look quickly in the mirror without switching on the light. My face showed gaping holes, a shadow on my nose. Like how white goes bright under ultraviolet light, like the Vaseline glass. I realized I hadn't brushed my teeth and found some lurid mouthwash in the mirrored cupboard over the sink. I took as big a mouthful as I could and spat it out almost immediately. I smoothed the outline of my hair. I didn't bother to rinse the purple mouthwash down the drain. I didn't bother to close the bathroom door behind me. From the hall, I could see Graves standing by his truck. He was wearing a long-sleeve t-shirt with some band name on the arm. I cringed. As if sensing this, he turned around to go back to the truck and pull out a flannel shirt. He put it on, buttoning it halfway. His truck was newly painted, a darker red. There was a scratch of the old shade on the hood.

"Why did you paint it red?" I asked, coming into the light.

"Stop. You're walking on your leg."

"Oh, yeah, I forget." I held the door open with my hip on the side of my good leg.

He laughed and started towards me. "It needed a paint job. It's all I had. I'd given up—until I met you." He came beside me and put two hands behind my legs as if he was about to lift me over his shoulder.

"What are you doing?"

"Carrying you back inside."

"Put me down. I need to get the keys."

"Where are they?"

"In my bike basket." He straightened up and took my hand, leading me around to the other side of the truck.

"Stand there on the grass," he ordered, flicking open the back hatch. He climbed up and said my name as he lifted off an olive tarp. Underneath was a large dirty shovel, some mud, and my bike. He pulled it out and set it on the ground before jumping down. "Margot," he said again. "Where are the keys?"

I pointed to the basket still lined with my bandanna, almost the same red as the truck. He bent down to untie its edges. The key ring fell on the ground beside four bags of snacks. "You like gummy bears," he remarked.

"Don't you?" He nodded and gathered up the things, leaving the bike on its side. He walked towards me and smiled as a way of asking permission.

"So, you've given up since you got here?" I put my arms around his neck to anchor myself, as he went to lift me.

"Until I met you," he said again. It made me feel good but uneasy. I said, "What does that mean?"

"I like you. I'm curious about you."

"No, what happened to make you give up?"

"Give up?"

"You said that you had—"

"Oh, yeah?" He asked a question where there had been one and put me down on the front steps. I pushed open the door. He silently followed me inside.

"You met me for fifteen minutes while I was bleeding in a cemetery," I said.

"It's a good start to a story."

"A vampire story."

"Whatever, yeah. How's your leg? What did they say?" he asked.

"It's fine. The doctor seemed as shocked as you that I didn't feel much of anything."

"I want to talk to you about that."

"Okay, um, do you want a drink? The kitchen's a mess. We can go out back or I can bring it to the living room. It's just down that hall to the left."

"I should help you."

"No, really. I'm fine. It will take me a moment to unlock the liquor," I said, holding up the key ring. "Go look at the view." I pointed to the left.

"Is this your house?"

"No." I didn't know whether to offer any more information. He laughed. "I will tell you everything in a little. Go."

I watched him leave. The dark blue plaid of his shirt clashed with the orange room ahead. "Insane," I heard him say to himself.

"It's not mine," I said quietly to myself. I stood paralyzed, watching him, a stranger becoming smaller down the corridor. Then I walked back to the second door and tried all of the keys until one worked. There was a small fridge-freezer within the larger concrete room, and inside that were several frozen bottles of vodka.

"Holy shit," I heard from the other room, and assumed he'd come upon the artwork across from the entryway. It made me think about the acclimatizer I'd noticed hidden behind the large television screen. I let him go on. Door #2. Key #2. Every imaginable kind of liquor. I picked up one of the vodkas and brought it to the kitchen counter. I went to the other closet and took out two of the neon glasses. Both were goblets with palm-size cups. I went to the main freezer and took out ice. It went yellow as it settled into the drink. I walked towards him, one glowing glass in each hand.

He watched me from where he'd settled at the bottom of the pit underneath a blue painting. His eyes surveyed my leg, moving in full range. There was no attempt to help me as I lumbered slowly down to join him, trying not to spill our vodka. "Here," I said, proffering a luminous cup. Viewed through the rim of my own glass, my bandages looked to be stained an unfortunate urine-brown. I kept my eyes averted from his same calm stare. I could feel it sweeping me up and down. My legs to my face to my chest to my legs and back again. I sat down next to him and put an orange cushion between us. I could smell him.

"So, what happened at the hospital?" He made eye contact. I looked up and out the window to avoid it, taking a sip of vodka. It was quick and cold. I bit down on my lip. His eyes went to my chin and my hand flew to meet them, covering the slight bruising. He edged closer and bent his neck, taking one of my hands in his and pushing the other away.

"Stop," I said. It felt like he was casing me. Looking for information to log. His eyes not unlike those of the other parties at an audition. My eyes went back to him, asking "Do I fascinate you?" Speaking my discomfort aloud, seeking attention. His eyes moved to the bandage on my leg. I smelled him again. "They did some kind of mini-surgery."

"Did it hurt?" he asked.

"No." I felt confused by my attraction to him. His interest in me. To make noise seemed better than the silence and staring. "Yeah, they probably should have given me something—ketamine?" I paused to see his reaction. He was shaking his head. "They asked me about my levels of pain and I kept telling them, 'Zero.'"

"I can't believe this. The chances are so small."

"Chances?"

"You have congenital analgesia."

"You're bad at flirting."

He kissed me, and then yanked my head back hard by my hair. I bit down. His hand to face; eyes to hand; yes. "That hurt."

I looked down. He was still staring.

"So, what do I have again?"

He was teasing me, like a boy in the playground. "Opioids could treat that."

"What?" I tried to follow and play along. Wit, Josephine always said. "They haven't worked yet."

"So you know?"

"Know what?" I asked.

"About your problem?"

"My problem?"

"It's very rare. You were born with an insensitivity to pain."

"I cry every day."

"Physical pain."

"I don't even know when something happens to me. I know *that*."

"Fuck," he said.

"What?"

"It's so crazy. I studied this in school."

"Yeah, yeah, you went to med school."

"No, I mean it was my specialty. I was trying to figure out a way to—"

"What are you talking about? Your specialty? You talk some nonsense, mister."

"No, really." He put down his empty glass on the orange floor and it disappeared into the carpet. I felt uneasy, as if this moment was significant but I didn't know how to be in it. His intensity was heavy on me. He kissed me again and I kissed him back because I didn't know what else to do. It seemed like some elaborate flirtation that batted my physicality back and forth. And then, we were both undressed. Surveyed from above: two unfamiliar bodies, one much taller than the other. And when he was on top of me, all that could be seen was a ring of hair, like an icon's halo, a static burst around his head. I didn't see him looking at me, not breaking eye contact. Instead I closed my eyes and imagined all of this from above.

And then he finished and lay still inside of me. His head now lowered. My upturned face in full view, the brown hair on the back of his heavy head to its right, like a two-faced creature. Only his ass and legs, spread arms holding out mine, a double wingspan. My bandage covered by his thigh. He stayed inside me for what could have been . . . minutes. The light out of the North window had changed. Hours. I had never felt so connected and disengaged.

What's your name? I couldn't bring myself to ask. It should have been offered. He had introduced me to my disorder, finally given it a name.

XXVII

When I woke up that morning, all I could think about was him. I had fallen asleep in the middle of the pit and he had left me where I lay. It was not about his eyes, voice, smell, or even the diagnosis, but about how full I'd felt. Unlike with the Director, whose gaze was always on his own movements, looking at himself sticking his fingers in my ass, absurdly proud of his mastery. Graves had found me bleeding like an animal in the woods, and everything he'd done for me and to me since that moment had been done with a cool, tender calm. And he'd known all about me, about how I worked. I tried to reason myself out of immature romanticism. Destiny is a stupid word. Josephine liked to use it. My mother would always tell her to quit it when she talked about the world that way. Hearing her mother believe in predetermination was for her the most painful thing. I never understood it, her anger when it happened. Once, when I was young, I overheard Josephine saying: "Godlessness. Name your next band that."

"You have no moral compass," my mother said.

"And you do? Leaving your family life like that."

"I didn't leave Margot, I left Steve. You don't understand. I didn't want to die in some . . ."

"Something stable?"

"Exactly. I would like *not* to die in something stable. There are other ways to live a life."

"You're proselytizing nonsense."

"Only you proselytize."

"Because I can't sing."

"Neither can I, really."

"I don't shout either."

"Maybe you should."

I rubbed my eyes and lifted myself out to go down the hall to the window. No truck, but the bicycle still on the ground. Where could he have had to go in a hurry, this graveyard man who was no longer a medical professional? I was naked. His absence felt violent because the intimacy had been so tender. I walked to the kitchen to get some water.

No pain in my leg, of course, and when I looked down the bandage was gone. I imagined it stuck to some part of Graves. He would drop it in the car before he got out wherever it was he had gone. Before I made it to the sink, that faraway sink, I turned back to the living room to check for the soiled fabric, though I was sure it had left with him.

Strange how thirsty I was, and dizzy. I felt in need of release, but nothing came except laughter. And I shut that off as soon as it began to sound. I reached my arms out to touch each side of the hallway with a finger, as if suspended there, trying to make myself breathe as my chest grew tight.

There in the kitchen beside the sink was a piece of paper, with the dirty bandage folded next to it. The sheet had come from one of the notebooks in the drawer. "Congenital analgesia," it said, and below that, in big capital letters: "CIPA." A script left after a house call. Fuck a doctor, get a diagnosis. I would probably never hear from him again.

I started to run the faucet and it coughed out brown. When it ran clear I cupped my hand and splashed water on my face. I could see my ass in the window behind me. It was maybe unwise to walk around the house naked. So many clear or reflective surfaces. I went upstairs for the first time in a week to find fresh clothes.

When I came back down, I had on a white t-shirt and black lace underwear I'd brought with me. My pants were in the living room somewhere. My wound had broken open, a small fissure in the crust. "Give it air," Josephine always said.

It was the first morning I hadn't thought about the Director or wondered if he was with the other woman. And then I thought of my mother. I sat on the metal chair by the back window and tried her again, holding tightly to a glass of water. Voicemail. I had to call Josephine. The uneasiness in my stomach rose as bile to my mouth. The distance had been helpful until it meant forgetting the bad.

Josephine picked up. "Margot, how are you?"

"I'm fine."

"You had a guest last night?"

"What?" I felt haunted by how she always seemed to know.

She corrected herself. "I just assumed maybe you did as I didn't get a response from you."

"Oh. You texted?"

"Anyway, tell me."

"I am worried about my mother. You've been so evasive and I really feel—"

She interrupted. "I'm sorry, Margot. I didn't want to tell you over the phone." My stomach fell as I remembered the same opener three months after my childhood dog died. I'd been away at school.

"Oh my God." I wanted to put down the phone, but she kept talking.

"J. found her in the doorway of their hotel room. They think it was brought on by some benzos and then—"

"They *think*?" I said. "How about this is the third time she's tried."

"It wasn't a try this time."

"You're an asshole." I had always wanted to say that to her. She hung up.

I dropped the glass and sank to the floor, hard. The kitchen wasn't carpeted but the glass didn't break, it just rolled away from my body. The floors in this house were strange. I still hadn't put on my pants. *My mother hung herself. Hanged? Hung?* I pressed my eyelids together and bit down, tasting metal. My head dropped and I let it hang heavy over my crossed legs, my arms wrapped around my thighs. My left hand felt for something and found it. I dug my nails in. It gave way. I rocked back and forth. There were no tears. I looked down and saw a thin line of blood oozing from where I'd pierced the hardened skin on my leg. A pale papery layer had formed at the edges of the wound. Maybe it would get infected. Or maybe the air would make it heal faster. *I need air.*

I was having trouble breathing again. The musk that overlaid the garbage smell had become nauseating. I pressed my heels into the ground to try and hold fast. Fuck. I tasted last night's vodka and, for a moment, Graves. I felt again for the scab with my hand, nervous compulsion. Dug a nail in again. Fluid. I got up to fetch paper towels, then slid back down. The soft tissues stuck, absorbed into the pocks. Somehow I pushed myself up and out the back door.

It must have been freezing, but I couldn't tell. My bare legs shook a little from something. The grief came in waves. Part of it was guilt at the relief. The relief of knowing for certain what I had already known; of hanging up on Josephine; of being alone without much attachment. Of not wanting any, except now with Graves.

I didn't want to form attachments like Josephine did, through control and manipulation. People needed her because they worried what she might know, a kind of pathological blackmail hidden in social dynamics. She was always watching. Surveillance everywhere.

Lucy once told me that there were cameras installed all around the Montana house, because her father had been paranoid about intruders. Standard reclusive artist mania. Josephine was like this for her own reasons. Lucy liked to side with Josephine. Defend her. They'd met and become instant pals. This happened with Josephine. She was seductive, animal-like, with her dancer's body and quiet aggression.

They'd exchanged numbers and texted all the time. I didn't understand.

A grandmother who still shape-shifts to find affinities with her targets. I felt a little like Graves had contrived this somehow, for it was impossible for us to be so fated. Standard reclusive artist mania? Josephine told me once, "Destiny can lie in not having a future." I wanted to call her back and tell her she'd landed on her daughter's destiny. She always knew. And she hadn't saved her. I hadn't either. My father was the only one she would ever really listen to, and that was only after the couple ended their commitment. So many discordant parts.

As Graves told it: my version was in the body. What you see signals pain, but I feel none. In time, I would see that his was the pathology of disconnection, emotional avoidance, covert grandiosity. Josephine had this, too. I will be the matriarch controlling the family, deciding what things are told, what details revealed. Really just a hyped-up version of a press agent.

I tried to think of something to take my mind off myself. The problem was that I was in that place to limit the distractions. Trying for this detachment wasn't unusual, I reassured myself, it was my goal. *This is why I'm here.* So I just kept looking. I walked right out the door, to find something, anything. And then I remembered the small house in the back.

Lucy had told me about this little building, her father's studio. When she was young and visiting him there, she'd sit by the window playing trains. He would be typing or taking calls or screening films, sometimes getting down on the floor beside her to move the boxcar. Whenever Lucy talked about her father, her face would turn off. Only for a moment, but it was clear, something behind her eyes had been unwired, untied. She loved him so much. I always thought it was because she knew so little about him. Behind the scenes. She said he liked to talk about his time in Paris, in France, whenever he'd had too much to drink. The liquor closet lock and its key.

I guess I had kept the studio a secret from myself, something to turn to when I'd exhausted everything else. My phone buzzed and I looked down to check the call log. Those missed in red. Then, ten, eleven out, to Rosemom. Graves. Rosemom. Josephine. Spam Risk.

I paused, thinking I saw a light on in the studio. Could someone be living there? A blow-in without a home, like me. Another pity-guest of Lucy's. The flash again, late Montana light off metal, like the living room. The same cycle of turning on and off a lamp.

There, in the window, reflective panes in front of brown curtains, I saw myself: naked legs and no shoes. The cold hadn't registered, but if I drew my attention back to my body I could feel something slick on the underside of my foot, what the rust maple had shed that morning.

I bent down and peeled the leaf off my skin where it had attached like a starfish. There were scuff marks at the bottom of the door. It was painted black over a blistered gray. It seemed to be the only dark-colored thing apart from the sky. The trees were bright, the grass wild and long, soaked and thriving. I tried to push the door inwards, but it wouldn't budge. Then I twisted and pulled the handle, which gave until it caught again on an old metal bar lock. I was poorly prepared for this venture.

I ran back inside to find the key ring. It made sense that this would be a job for that one copper key. When I went back outside, I was careful to hop over the slimy red leaves. As I went for the hole, my shaking hands made the key difficult to maneuver. When I pulled it back out, cobwebs like those that filled the high corners of the house came out on the rod. I pushed and the door gave way to a whole curtain of webs, which I walked directly through. Some papers lifted in the breeze that accompanied me and blew one by one to the floor. Any other day and this would have been a grand discovery. A magic place. I stepped into the studio.

It was like the life-size dioramas in the period rooms at museums. Everything arranged as if someone had left for a cigarette break and would be back, even forty years later. Untouched. "You'll see all the film critic shit in the converted toolshed," Lucy said when she gave me the virtual tour. "The main house is wired as best it can be in remote Montana, the back very much isn't." No Wi-Fi, bless.

The space seemed much bigger inside than it appeared when viewed from the windows of the main house. In the middle was a desk with legs like a compass. All along the back wall, cardboard boxes labeled "16mm" in thin black marker. Near them, a smaller desk with the same pointy legs. On top of that stood a projector, grey and dusty, plugged into the outlet by a long thick cord. There was an antique Moroccan rug with faded orange and brown stripes, frayed edges, and cigarette burns. Piles of books were stacked against the facing wall, three thick. No bookshelves, just towers all along the perimeter. And next to them, half the height, the VHS cassettes in their slide-in boxes. I nearly tripped over a large leather cushion on the floor, which caused me to look down and see a little blood running down my leg to the floor. I tore a piece of graph paper from a French-looking notebook and stuck it to the wetness.

Every ten stacks there were loose, sleeveless tapes, most black, some yellow. There were two machines labeled "VCR," one connected to a projector via a blue auxiliary cord. A desk lamp sat on top of a stack of books. There was a chair next to it, occupied by three larger books. A piece of paper was held to the main desk by some kind of award, an Emmy or Oscar-type sculpture, but in the shape of a double swan forming a heart. The wall had been painted white many times over in the rectangular area where the projector beam hit. It was an old machine with a simple on/off switch, a tiny grey triangle pushed in or out on the side. I felt something by my foot and saw a loop of metal staked to the floor. And looked up to the ceiling, where there was a pull-down screen operated by a red and white string.

Lucy told me that her father had been part of the jury for the cancelled Cannes festival of 1968. He must have been very young then, but the story tracked with the boxes of press kits and reels, all labeled in typewriter. Sharp letters spelling titles like *Petulia* and *Peppermint Frappé*. There were printed photos with men in scrum formation and old microphones above a hedge of white hydrangea.

Men in blazers on a stage. A glamorous woman strolling with a short man along the Croisette.

I thought of my mother and felt sick. Coughed, unsettling dust into the air. I picked up my phone to call her, to hear her voice on the voicemail message. And then decided not to. What had she used? She always had a roll of thick black velvet ribbon with her when she traveled. What kind of chair had she kicked? Was it a stool? Hotels don't usually have stools. The pills didn't work the last two times. Why hadn't Josephine told me? An act of mercy. Rope. Chair. Pillbox. Funeral. I slid to the floor and hugged my knees as I had before, head bent, rocking. When I stood up, a piece of paper fluttered to the ground, a round stigmata mark at its center. I left it lying there and the door unlocked as I walked back to the main house.

XXVIII

Graves texted me. "How are you?" When I didn't answer right away, he sent a photo of a book he'd been reading. "This is good." Strangely, it was the autobiography of a jazz bassist in which my grandfather appeared. Another odd coincidence—as if he'd done his research. How? I hadn't answered for three hours because I had been sitting crying alone in the shed. This had wounded him enough to send another, somehow more dismissive text. "I hope your leg is okay and you are having a nice day."

I wrote back: "I need to learn more about what you told me." He answered immediately, "Should we meet soon?"

"Yes, please. When is best for you?"

"This evening."

Lucy rang, an hour before her usual call. In all the days up till then, she'd never once changed the time.

"Hey, what's wrong?"

"What do you mean?"

"You never call at this time."

"I walked out."

"Walked out?"

"I had a—I dunno—a sense you needed me?"

"Truly?"

"Yeah, it was weird."

"Where are you now?"

"I went to the bench around back and called you," Lucy said.

"Can you see the library? Are there leaves?"

"Margot."

"Okay, what?"

"Some of the things you've said to me the past few calls don't sit well."

"What do you mean?"

"You realize I've seen you with men before? You're addicted to people who ignore your needs."

"What about you?" I asked.

"Ay, the deflection, but also don't forget we met because of it."

"Because of what?"

"Because you asked me to move my protest from right next to your dressing room for that show and I refused," Lucy said.

"It wasn't much of a protest."

"That should have been your complaint, then. I can still see you in your silver catsuit, peeking around the door, sneering at me."

"You were sitting in front of my dressing room with signs and candles and I had to go on in ten minutes!"

"Neither here nor there. And here we are. Listen. I think maybe you were fucked up by your mother being so neglectful when you were small. You don't expect anyone

139

to meet your needs, so you think if you can actively pursue that, it will transmute into what you want."

"I don't follow."

"No one can hurt you. Not if you *want* them to."

"Does volition negate intention?"

"Something like that?"

"Are you saying I don't want to be loved? Come on."

"Something like that."

"How do you explain all my combusted relationships?"

"Adrenaline. Intimacies that became hits, seeking highs. Addiction. Like drugs, which never really cut it for you. It runs in your family."

"So much does."

"Addiction, depression."

"All the classics."

"Margot. Things can be real without conflict."

"Can they?"

"Trauma can be transformed. Someday, even generations later. Someone decides it won't be the excuse for their own bad behavior."

"A relationship without conflict, though?"

"I don't mean without conflict. Without, like, *abuse.*"

"How will I know?"

"When what was destructive becomes generative."

"Don't trust your feelings."

"Margot!"

"Hahhahahaha."

XXIX

Graves's truck had a very particular hum I could hear from down the driveway. I had managed to find pants and some frozen pizzas, and to turn the oven on before his arrival. I'd put on Josephine's necklace. When he came inside, I noticed for the first time how tall he was. He wore shabby brown dress shoes and a button-down over a white t-shirt. "Nice to see you," he said quietly, and his eyes dropped to my gold choker.

"You too, come in, sit down." I closed the door behind him and held my arm out to the hallway, playing the hostess. He walked ahead and I followed, pleased with what I'd set up. In the center of the pit was a tortoiseshell tray I'd found behind a door.

"You look cute." His delivery made it seem only half a compliment. For some reason everything he said felt barbed. We barely knew each other. Holding back would have been best, yet also risky. I could lose his interest, and I needed his knowledge. I'd never felt that way with anyone so quickly. Another audition. Was I worthy of his attention? It would be hard to sustain the drama of our first graveside meeting.

"Do you eat pizza?"

"Yeah, of course."

"I'm sorry. I don't really cook and I'm still figuring my way around everything here. You have to see what I found out back."

"Should we have a drink first?"

"Sure, same as before?" He nodded. I went to the kitchen to get the glasses.

When I came back, he stared at my face, searching. "You look like you've been crying."

"Crying? No." He took the goblet while that calm stare didn't waver from my face. I looked down, pretending to rearrange the silverware and paper napkins on the tray.

"You know I have you in my phone as Graves." He laughed. Offered nothing.

"That works."

"Where did you say you were from?"

"I, uh, was in New York before this."

"Oh, me too."

"Really?"

"Yeah, my family has a place there." I didn't want him to know how young I was. He seemed much older. I was so attracted to him. There were signs that he knew things about me. Small allusions that made me feel crazy. Always said in that steady way—offering little, seeking more in return.

"I've been asking around about your friend Lucy."

"Oh?"

"Yeah, seems like everyone was a big fan of her parents. They sound cool." He avoided asking anything directly. To do so would mean that I could ask him things.

"I finally went into her father's studio yesterday. It's in the back, there's a projector and all these reels." He appeared excited for a second, then collected himself into his calmness.

"I went to film school."

"I thought you were a doctor."

"Yeah, frustrated film school doctor."

"Oh."

"Seemed a little narcissistic to think I should be making movies, as if somehow that would help the world."

"Logical next step: brain surgeon," I said. He laughed. The kitchen timer rang and I hoisted myself up to get the pizza.

I brought it out on a clear plastic tray. As I approached, Graves could see through the bottom to the cheap crust. "You burnt it a little."

"Oh." We were silent for a few minutes, sitting there eating. "Tell me," I said, "how many lives have you saved."

He cleared his throat. "I don't really look at it like that. I mean, hundreds of operations since my residency?"

"I don't really know how it works."

"What did you study?"

"Theatre Arts and Performance Studies. I'm an actress." He laughed. "Why is that funny?"

"It's fated, in a way. You can't feel, so you pretend to feel."

"I feel fine. Emotions, I mean."

"The circuitry for physical and emotional pain is the same."

"I don't follow."

"You have broken neuroreceptors. And I mentioned opioids before, you know that after emotional pain—rejection—the brain sends out pain-killing opioids. Well, it's much more complicated. Affects, cognitive function."

"I don't know what any of that means."

"I wonder if we could play with how it affects arousal?"

"Sorry?" This comment made me feel uncomfortable.

"I'm just thinking out loud. Did you know that deliberately inflicted pain hurts more?"

"How do they know that?"

"It's been studied. If you saw me try to trip you and you fell, it would be more painful. Well, not *you*, but you know what I mean."

"I will keep that in mind." The questing intelligence made me uneasy.

"I like looking at you," he had said when we were fucking. And at that moment it felt good, optical devotion. He didn't seem connected to his body. Instead he was wielding his sex like a weapon, just holding himself there. He never came, so far as I could tell. I kept this rattling at the back of my mind. When he finished his slice of pizza, he got up to clear the tray. I still had some on my plate.

"Stop. I'll do that."

"No, no. I want to look around." It was an odd admission. I didn't bother to argue.

When he came back, he started on my parents. "So, your dad was in that punk band—"

"Wait, where is this coming from?"

"I'm fascinated by you. So mysterious and kind of glamorous. What's the thing around your neck?"

"Was that a compliment?" He laughed and lifted his shoulders. "It belonged to Alice Coltrane. She gave it to my grandmother." He didn't seem impressed. I felt bad at having dropped the name. I should have been humbler. His eyes said so.

"You've told me nothing about you," I countered.

"We have a lot of time."

"We do?"

"Yes," he said, touching the small of my back. "You know, so many music terms are pejorative, from hate speech. Jazz was jazz, punk was what they called the guy who was passed around in prison."

"I actually heard that before, from my mother."

My head dropped. He noticed. "I'm sorry."

"Don't be sorry." I knew that if he'd looked me up, he would have seen that her death had been announced weeks before. I checked the computer after I spoke to Josephine. Before I looked up my disorder. Unable to rely on my family, I could have found out the death of my own mother from a Google alert.

XXX

After we cleared the rest of the dinner, I led Graves out back. He had to duck because of his height.

"*Cinéma du corps*," he said.

"What?"

"Nothing." He pointed at the projector. "There's a film in there."

"Oh, right. You and your film school." I switched the machine on. In the dark, I could see the light on the wall.

"Let's try it," he said, moving a metal bar to the side. It coughed a little and then flashed on. He sat down on the edge of orange carpet and motioned me to sit beside him. The title sequence showed scratches, radio feedback. An old cinema in a Montana shed.

And then the square of wall showed men sitting around a table, speaking Czech, inspecting a fire ax. It had been kept in a leather box, with a sunken velour cushion made to its contours: a wooden handle with a steel hatchet on one side, a sharp hook on the other.

"Exactly what we came for," Graves said jokily in my ear.

Cut to a ballroom where a party is being prepared. There will be a raffle with prizes like a pig's head, a porcelain plate, a stuffed toy. Numbered raffle tickets. A dangling banner of firemen saving people goes up in flames. About seven minutes in, the credits, big serif letters the same color as the carpet. Acute accents and diacriticals: Miloš Forman, director. Then, some *Curb Your Enthusiasm* circus music and the title: *Hoří, má panenko*. I didn't know how one would pronounce this, but to my surprise Graves looked at me and said it aloud.

"You speak Czech?"

"Yes, and a few other languages."

"You're a brain surgeon who speaks Czech?"

"Trauma surgeon—neurosurgeon."

"Okay." The soundtrack continued even when we stopped paying attention. He turned to me and I knew what was going to happen. Lucy would have loved it: Czech New Wave in the background, fucking on her dad's beloved Moroccan rug.

He didn't come. We lay there as one, watching the rest of the movie. "Did you feel that?" he asked.

"Why don't you come?"

"What do you mean?" He laughed.

"Did you come?"

"I think so. I don't know," he said. "Why do you want me to?"

"You don't know?" He didn't answer. His eyes said that my questions were too intimate. Which felt wrong, because they were about lack of intimacy. In response he hugged me from behind, one arm across my body, holding my hand.

"Oxytocin," he said.

"What?"

"When you orgasm."

"Okay?"

"Bonds you to things."

"Right, biology. We want connection," I said.

"Not all of us. Some people want control."

"Are you hungry?" I asked, thinking I should.

"No, we just had pizza. Let's change the reel."

"Do you know how?"

"I'm a lot older than you."

"Ancient, like this equipment."

He laughed and got up, pulling his pale blue shorts back on. "You do think I'm old," he said.

"Anyone over thirty is old."

"Right."

"Do you have any kids?"

He laughed again. "No, do you?"

I shook my head. "I have an IUD." I wasn't sure what he was asking.

"Okay."

"Do you play sports?" I didn't know where that question came from.

He looked embarrassed as he unclipped the reel. "I like sports."

"Like tennis?"

"No. Like ice climbing."

"Oh. Adrenaline."

"And you?"

"According to you: a mutant."

"Also true."

"What did you call it?"

"CIPA."

"See-pa?"

"Congenital insensitivity to pain and anhidrosis. Also HSAN IV, hereditary sensory and autonomic neuropathy type IV."

"You *are* a doctor."

He lay down beside me again.

"You're lucky you never got an infection. I can't believe no one tested you or noticed."

"My parents were too busy making music."

"Right. I used to listen to your dad's records."

"You *are* old."

Then I said, "My mother hanged herself in a hotel room a few weeks ago."

It just came out. I couldn't help myself. And lying together made it easier to talk. I had experienced this in reverse already. The Director told me about his indiscretions only when undressed in bed. Naked and warm, he could manipulate me.

"I'm sorry, Margot," Graves said. Pulling himself away from me and crossing his arms against his chest.

"Why did you pull away."

"I didn't," he said. The calmness shaded into contempt.

"I'm sorry," I said back to him.

He said nothing and went back to the machinery. "This one is called *Peppermint Frappé*," he said. "Both this and the Czech film were supposed to be in competition in

Cannes when it was cancelled in '68." More dust billowed in the air as he unrolled some of the film.

"How do you know that?"

"Film studies, but, yeah, it also says it clearly over there. Seems like this guy was on the jury that year, maybe?" He stretched out the clear film and held it up away from the cloud it released. "Back to your body," he said, as if it was a natural segue. "You have defective NTRK1, the tyrosine kinase receptor doesn't work. Also, I assume you don't sweat?"

"How did you know *that*?"

"Or feel the cold. It goes with the disease. You can't feel pain or temperature, really. It's surprising you can orgasm." Full detachment as he said it. He started the machine and came back to sit next to me on the floor.

"Are you cold?" he asked, performing chivalry.

"That's not very funny." The movie started to play. This one was about a man who becomes obsessed with the wife of his friend. Graves said it was about "repression and desire." I played dumb. He liked to talk like he was educating me. "The protagonist is a bourgeois doctor with 'ideas' about a female-object."

"You are my film teacher now," I said.

"Really?" He said it in a strange voice.

"Sure," I said. "Why do you say it like that?" I'd put my shirt back on.

"You used to act, right?"

"Still do. I'm taking a break."

"Can we do some experiments?"

"That sounds sinister."

"I want to see if we can teach your body about sensation."

"Why?"

"Like an experiment. To regulate emotion, fear, threats, in fixed time."

"Fixed time? I'm not an object for your fascinated investigation."

"No?" There was a shift in his eyes, maybe a dilation. His attention felt better than anything had in a long time. He kept his hand on my leg, just below the cut. And then he got up and left again.

Ten minutes later, he texted me. "I am so happy to have found you." We made plans that evening to meet every other day around 5 p.m., or whenever the sun set on the back house.

The meetings carried on for two months before the shift happened. It was a merger of two people who had found each other in an unlikely place. Like that pop song from fifteen years ago. Graves idealized me in my disorder. All his cold complications were interesting to me, a distraction from my confused grieving. Days and then weeks passed when I didn't think of the Director. A double shot of tragedy and sex to get over an abandonment. I couldn't hold all these concepts in my head. My poor mother.

Graves told me there is a thing, like the *cinéma du corps*, called the cinema of attractions. A term coined by a guy named Tom Gunning. Something like you present a series of images to tell a story, without worrying too much about the words. "Exhibitionist confrontation rather than diegetic absorption." He brought up a short movie on

151

YouTube with his phone: "How It Feels to Be Run Over," shot in 1900 by the Hepworth Manufacturing Company. A motorcar crawling towards imminent collision with the screen.

XXXI

Graves's ad hoc curriculum worked with what was at hand. We had *24 Hours in the Life of a Woman, Anna Karenina, Bandits in Milan, Charlie Bubbles, The Red and the White.* They were all dated 1968. There was a graphic printed on the faded pieces of paper that lined the bottom of the box. It had the digits "2" and "1" in red and orange arranged like a sun, 21212121212121212121. Below, "*21e Festival International du Film: Le Rendez-vous Mondial du Cinéma. Cannes 1968. Du 10 au 24 Mai.*" And then, taped below that: "*Interrompu par solidarité avec les étudiants et les travailleurs, le Festival de Cannes est annulé.*"

I knew that *annulé* meant cancelled, because of an old French Vogue subscription that I could no longer have sent to my US address. It had happened the same year that cancel culture became a thing. Two reasons. One in solidarity with the mission, the other when you were a threat to a mission.

In the same box, there were other films with the label, a font similar to that on the poster and a small disclaimer, something in French like *for research purposes only.* These prints had come out long after the original release date. My mother found new fame at the end, too.

I wondered if the Director had read the news about my mother. Whether it had made him pause. I hadn't expected that to be the way I first showed up for him. In death, in the sensational part of the news.

I thought of how my mother had refused to shop at the A&P by Josephine's place, because of the bright lights by the frozen food.

My mother would first come in images without sound. No talking, no music, no noise. Most often, she came as color. Or colors, like on the fabric of bus seats. Then, a crash and breakthrough sound: her voice fighting with someone on the phone. It was always the same rhythm when it was my father. Soft, soft, yell, soft, silence. The tactic was him knowing her, and her conceding in their language. She was bad with emotion. I saw my father hold her once and her bend then.

She was never affectionate towards me, but I still felt her behind my eyes the way I had as a child, when she watched me fall asleep. No cuddling or handholding, not even a story, but she would sit there next to me and watch. I felt safe this way, with someone watching me. Graves did it when we fucked. Attention on my body. Never caving to the chemicals of love.

Even so, he wanted me to succumb to him, so he could puppeteer my sensations. I read a book once that said psychologically sound sex was a way of showing gratitude to your partner. This was never how I experienced it. With Graves, the exchange became a way for someone to ignore my needs. Without physical pain, this masochistic ecstatic love is impossible. The boundaries don't exist to break down. Is it still as dangerous when you lack the receptors to warn you?

Graves never brought her up again after that first day. He never asked how I was processing her death. Never a care for my interior life, that which he couldn't X-ray to see. Multiple texts every day, though, asking where I was, when there was nowhere to go. Sometimes when I didn't answer he would text again. The second message passive and aggressive. I learned his rhythms quickly, but it was hard to determine what would or would not upset him. The ratio stayed constant. Four out of five interactions, everything was fine. But sometimes he would rage. Every other day, we ate pizza in the orange pit and then went to the back house to watch movies.

One of the days, we watched *Petulia*, and it was the coolest movie I'd ever seen. Meaning cold. Whatever desire was present was expressed in absence. It opens at a benefit where a beautiful married woman flirts with an aloof doctor. She tells him her husband is a naval engineer, asks if he needs a boat. In the grand hall, she's shaking it for a hospital her father-in-law supports, shilling her husband's useless credentials. They end up at a robotic hotel, nothing is consummated. The "Pepsi generation" is mentioned. Someone says they just want to be able to feel like everyone else. The children of the doctor's divorce are only shown being taken by one parent or the other to somewhere like the zoo. A nurse in a hospital (the one bankrolled by the father-in-law) makes a snide racist comment about a boy

Petulia has injured with her fancy car. She too ends up in the hospital. And delivers a final zinger that lets the audience know she is aware—even the mastermind—of her kookiness, all along conscious of its perverse power. Graves said he didn't like the film. It made him very uncomfortable.

Then, one day, all of a sudden, for twenty-four straight hours, he was attentive, responsive. He even finished inside me.

XXXII

"I feel like I've known you forever," he said the next evening after we'd fucked on the floor. He'd come again, and the sound he made was . . . unsettling. And now this.

"That's lame."

"I just mean that I feel complete devotion. We must have met before, past life? It just feels familiar. Your whole thing."

"My whole thing?"

"Yeah, your whole magical thing."

"Don't be absurd." These sudden declarations made me uneasy.

"I love you, Margot. I love you." He said it twice, as if feeling it out.

"Because I am statistically an anomaly?"

"Yes and no."

"You still haven't told me what you're doing here."

He looked at me too long before answering. "I needed some time, to be alone." I wanted to ask from who or what, but his stare cautioned against it. "You know what, I should go," he said. It was very confusing. He pulled on his shorts.

"Yeah, you should."

"You are *so* intense," he said. "I hope you're okay." Detached.

"I am. *I am*," I repeated back to him. He nodded twice and left me sitting naked on the floor. His shoes would be where he always left them, at the threshold. I watched through the window as he opened the main house door and walked into the kitchen.

I slept in the shed that night and woke up, uncharacteristically wet around my lower back, thinking I should have insisted he stay. Did I do something wrong? Why did he become so cold? The replay of thoughts started in the same space as the Director occupied. I didn't like going in there. For weeks I hadn't had to. Instead, sex and experiments. Films and discussions.

And then, like the wind, Graves changed.

XXXIII

I never allowed myself to look at the tabloid magazines at the corner store. They brought back memories of the photographers camped outside Josephine's house. And then, all I could think about was my mother. Looking online was always a mistake. Because she was famous, made more famous by her personal life. The disembowelment of a known person who commits suicide is different than that of your mother. These two people are not the same.

Fans don't mourn, they celebrate. New idolatry; her last years in a new biography. Someone wrote in the comments, "she could have at least waited until Margot was twenty-seven."

She never did get to learn how special I was, what was really wrong with me, and how she had made me that way. Soft, soft, yell, soft, silence was sometimes an argument about why they never could collaborate on anything that became successful.

My father didn't, couldn't, call. Sent the same emails. Josephine continued to call every day at the same time.

My father still signed every note with his first name. And Lucy, reliable, every day at 3 p.m. after her seminar.

I had messaged Graves not to come that morning, as I was going to ride into town and get some supplies at the convenience store. He didn't answer. I left my bicycle unlocked outside the shop because he'd told me no one ever stole anything there.

Back when I was in college, I had liked to steal. For the rush, really. Graves would get that. When summer came around, Lucy and I would steal from cafes along our path. I had a collection of cups and saucers and glasses with logos from all over. Lucy said her mother's collection of uranium glass was rivaled only by our stolen tableware.

I checked my phone to see if Graves had been in touch. Nothing. I tried calling and he didn't pick up. Days earlier he had called twice, three times a day. I texted him, "What's going on?" He didn't reply.

An hour later: "Hey sorry crazy day. I'm with a friend in town. Try you a little later? X"

He had no job, as far as I could tell. Except our experiments. No one ever came to visit him. He'd asked me to pick up one of those infrared thermometers so we could clock my temperature during the next session. I found some at the back of the store. Because it was an old corner store, there was also an ancient mercury model sucked tight on a blister pack, on sale for $4.99. I took the other kind and put it in my basket, grabbed some nuts and candy, and made my way to the front of the shop.

I saw a familiar drug dealer come in and then leave. He had come to 57 Plinth on one of my first days. I had found him through Lucy. That novelty quickly wore off. The thing about this town was that everything was available if I wanted it. But I had no withdrawal when I stopped. Felt nothing. For me, drugs were only ever about the ritual and camaraderie of the collective experience. It seemed different for other people. Same with sex.

The magazines were leering at me. I stole a quick peek: same screaming neon fonts next to the checkout. I tried to look straight ahead and not read the covers. I took out three bags of gummy bears and a packet of peanuts, for the cemetery blue jays, and put them on the conveyor belt. And then, the thermometer gun at the bottom of the plastic hatched carrier. The man behind the checkout didn't look at me, didn't care. I paid in cash. He flicked up the black plastic bar that held each denomination down. He couldn't be bothered to separate the ones from the fives. This made me uneasy, like the missing cows so many years ago. I left with my goods.

On the rare occasions there was someone else on the street, they usually averted their eyes when they saw me. The opposite of what I experienced with my father. I knew someone had spread the rumor that I came to this town because I was "sick," which meant contagious. But I wasn't that kind of sick. One of my diseases was both incommunicable and impossible to test for. The other was also incommunicable, but, I would learn, it could have been detected *in utero*. One was contagious, just not straight away. It takes time to infiltrate the existence of another body, to hijack intimacy.

I picked up my bike and put the goods in the basket. Guiding the handlebars, I walked along the main street.

Most of the businesses in town had no signage or lettering on the windows. The bait and tackle shop had a crude wooden fish out front, vaguely religious. There was no one around but the man smoking behind me.

"Bye-bye," the man said as he threw down his cigarette. Twice. Bye. Bye.

XXXIV

When I arrived home, Graves was waiting for me in the back house. I'd forgotten to lock the door. He'd left his brown shoes by the door. The same place as always. In three short months, we had made a misfit couple of ourselves. I left the snacks on the kitchen counter and brought the thermometer out back.

I found him going through a box of press materials. He looked up as I walked in.

"I found this interview—you should read it. This director says that she uses actors by negating them."

"That makes sense to me," I said.

"How so?"

"I mean I act from my imagination, not from observation." Pause. "You do the opposite, in a way."

"What do you mean?"

"You don't think about things that aren't in front of you. There's no romanticizing or accountability when you're off site. It's all about your needs, not imagining someone else's." He started to look angry. "Sometimes I will text you and it's like you don't even read the message, you reply to yourself."

He sucked in his breath and looked away. "Sorry I wasn't able to text you travel updates."

"Why? What could you possibly have been doing?"

"I don't want to fight, Margot. It's exhausting."

"This isn't fighting."

"Okay. You know, this kind of love you're looking for only exists in movies. I don't operate in these couple-unit things."

"What are we doing, then?"

"We like each other. We're attracted to each other. I don't know what the promise is."

"What?"

"Never mind."

"What are you talking about?"

"I'm trying to understand how we interact."

"Well, you don't act, you react."

"Could be true. I'm unsure when it comes to you."

"What?"

"You already said that."

"I feel like you're messing with my head," I said.

And then something that had never occurred to me suddenly jumped out. "Are you with someone?"

"So dramatic. I'm not keeping anything from you. I was in a fucked-up co-dependent thing with this insane woman. Miserable. She knew how to manipulate me. It was confusing."

"What do you mean. You're not with her anymore?"

"I don't really know what that means," and then his

mouth twisted. "Remember you telling me about your daughter-of theory?"

"Wait, do you still talk to her?"

"There's a connection, we text. I help her with her work."

"What?"

"Why do you seem so surprised. I have friends," he said. "You're making a big deal out of nothing. I want to show you something else that I found before you arrived."

"Yes?"

"Did you know Godard cast Alain Tanner's daughter in one of his movies. Look at this." He held up an issue of a movie magazine from the '80s: there was a picture of three cows staring back. Underneath it said, "Still from No Man's Land." He went on, "There's a story where Godard mocks him and says the cows have three different expressions, unlike the actresses."

"I like cows."

He laughed. "Okay." He came up beside me and put his hand between my legs. I let him and folded my shoulders over into his stomach, head turned sideways pressed against him. He picked me up and carried me to the orange rug. Started to undress me. My clothes were off, but he had kept his shirt on. He knelt down and put his hands under my ass, lifting it towards his face.

"You are so fucked up," I said, laughing. He slid one of his fingers inside of me from the back.

"What? Margot." His touch was off balance with the negation of his words. His calm black eyes wouldn't stop looking at me. I closed mine and bit down on my lip. His mouth followed his hand and he couldn't say anything anymore. I kept my eyes closed as he did it. There was a pause and he took his mouth away. I felt him stand up, heard him walk to the desk, open something, close it and come back. Time passed.

And I felt the wetness and rhythmic motion again. Only one of his hands, his left, was behind the right side of my ass. I was still half sitting up, my back exposed. He usually held fast with both hands when I began to move in time to him. There was nothing holding my left side. Without the restraint, I kicked him as I came. It happened very fast and then, when I opened my eyes and tried to put him inside of me, he was already gone.

"No, I want you," I said.

"Stay there, don't move." I listened to him. "Turn over onto your stomach. Close your eyes." He got up again and then I felt something on my back.

"What are you doing?"

"Nothing, just wait." And then he entered me from behind. I pulled myself open a little more to allow for it. It was enough to have him inside. His hands went down to my hips and we were in familiar formation. But something was different. And when I opened my eyes and turned my head I saw something new on his face.

"What's wrong?"

"Nothing, you're acting crazy." And there he was holding himself over me watching the back and forth. Staring at the part of my hip that went inward and up to my waist. Then, he stopped. Withdrew. Got up and put his clothes on.

XXXV

Later, he called and said he wanted to talk. He told me he found the coolness he had loved about me in the beginning a bit off-putting. That I was acting kind of lofty. He said he wasn't into that and wanted to know why I'd changed. I said I didn't know what he was talking about. I asked for examples and he had trouble providing any. I asked about his leaving so abruptly and he said he had no recollection of that. I hung up in tears.

I called Lucy and explained the situation. She had already warned me that everything was happening far too fast. That he was blowing too hot for it to last, that I should try to find out more about him. And now there was a long pause on the other end of the phone.

"Margot, I asked around about him."

"I asked you not to do that." Graves was always telling me that he didn't want anyone to know his deal, that I should be discreet about us. Lucy was the only other person I talked to.

"I had to, Margot. It's not good."

"What do you mean?"

"He had a very fucked-up relationship with some woman. And then something happened, and he was sacked. Got passed up for a promotion and flew into a rage."

"What?"

"He's not a super-well guy."

"People love to gossip."

"You're under some sort of spell . . . Again!"

"It's totally intense, and it's been kind of amazing."

"Margot."

"You'll meet him when you come. When are you arriving again?"

"I'm supposed to fly out at the end of the week. You're not listening to me."

"I know how people are. It's easy to make up stories surrounding someone like him."

"Margot, he's still with her."

"I know, they talk about work. He helps her."

"Margot. I mean it. I feel like I said similar things but it was less serious with the Director. You need to wise up. I know how painful it has been these last months, and I'm coming as soon as I can. I would never tell you anything just to fuck with you or make you sad. I really think you need to be careful."

"I'm fine." I felt myself getting angry. I wanted to tell her I was in love, but that sounded petulant and juvenile.

"Margot, I am very serious right now. The family friend I spoke to sounded creeped out by this guy. What does he really want? Well, I get that's a bad question. What else could he want but you out there in the middle of nowhere."

"I'm not sure he even registered my parents."

"Margot, that's not what I mean. I'll see you Friday." She cut the line.

XXXVI

It was normal for me not to shower every day, even every three days. My hair would stay wet forever in the air there, never dry. Some mornings I tried to sleep in but failed, because I couldn't figure out how to close the blackout blinds. Graves had become my entire focus: his lessons and my performances, our recordings and our screenings. We were playing at house, movie theater, and medical theater all at once.

The name Graves had stuck. He liked it. After we watched *Goto, Island of Love,* he started calling me Goto. He said it was the perfect diminutive of Margot. The movie was about a penal colony, shot in Marie and Pierre Curie's abandoned factory. Anti-authoritarian.

Goto and Graves.

I'd wear the same clothes for days. To be able to smell him once he was gone. He rarely slept over. I hadn't changed my clothes since he last left. When I took off my jeans and started the shower, I saw the wound on my leg held closed with a thick brown scar edged in white. The graveyard was a long time ago.

I pulled my sweater over my head and the undershirt clung to my back. I reached behind me with my left hand to try and feel why it was caught there. Stuck to something. I reached further, as far as I could, and felt a piece of tape. Over it, matted fabric, stiff and hardened. I tried to shake it free.

I walked into the bathroom backwards towards the mirror, pressing the light on with my right hand. At first it was difficult to angle myself properly, but I climbed on the step stool to sit on the marble base of the sink. And then, I saw.

My stomach fell. The back of my undershirt was soaked with blood. It had hardened into itself, the shirt material as a suture. There seemed to be some tape behind it.

I opened the drawer and pushed around some hairbrushes, looking for scissors. There was a nail clipper. I picked it up and tried to clamp down through the crusted fabric. It gave and I was able to peel off the shirt in two pieces. It made sense that I could have hurt myself and not felt it, but that wouldn't explain the tape.

I tried to recall any time in the past few days when I could have blacked out, but I hadn't drunk like that in months, and no longer took any kind of pills. I reached for my phone to look for Graves's number, to send him a picture and ask what he thought. As I was angling the phone to the mirror, I dropped it. The tape. Perfectly, surgically applied in a line, so the wound couldn't reopen if the fabric didn't hold.

I sank to the floor, head in hands, knees bent to either side. I thought about what he had said earlier. My mind went blank. All I could think to do was call him. I picked up my phone and pressed his name.

He declined the call.

XXXVII

I tried to sleep that night but didn't get anywhere. Lucy would arrive the next day. Graves never returned my call. I thought about putting Neosporin on my back, but my arms were so stiff and so tired, I didn't think I could reach.

Lucy would help me the following day.

Can you cause pain to someone who feels none?

Does it hurt to know he did it without telling me?

That old oath: do no harm.

He didn't hurt me.

I mean, he did, but.

Unable to rest, I decided to get up and return to the shed. We'd only gotten halfway through the last movie. He had become increasingly erratic in his demands and expressions. The calmness was mostly there, but more like a deadness now, which didn't tally with what he'd ask of me in sex. He would become irate at random moments, would have to hold himself back. I began to consider my safety.

I thought back to how he had said that the circuitry for physical pain was the same as for emotional pain.

Penetration the opposite of withholding. Patience and consistency, or manipulation and control. The way some filmmakers mismatch images and sound, he sometimes liked to mess with words and actions. He had the same line about music, that when lyrics and music didn't fit together it made for the most memorable kind of song. That melody was not created by notes. Part of the justification of American exceptionalism was that all the best songs were in American English. A total pseud, but even so, a lot of what he said could seem smart, complicated, interesting.

He denied responsibility for his own problems, arguing that the systems in our world encouraged emotional lives based on transactional gain. That revisionist history was what everyone used to feel okay, because no one could accept the world as it was. I heard all these statements in sound bites of exhaustion. People aren't bad; it's all just situations, hierarchies being presented to us, which we're invited to survive or not survive.

He once tried to explain the science behind why people experience emotion *differently*. He didn't account for outliers, whether freaks like me or anyone who was not beneath and below him. I came to see that even in his head-down, humble act, he felt we were all just in service to his research. He'd tried and failed for years to get the film collective he had founded off the ground. When he got drunk enough, he would rant about it.

I thought about what Lucy had said. Why did he care about me? What did we have in common? Only that my disorder matched his interest. And sex. Was he invulnerable to pleasure, knowing it would make it more difficult to cause pain?

He said he could never decide what he wanted, but waited for things to happen to him. A doctor in the ER does this, too. And no one can blame him. He was forever stripping blame away from individuals, even imaginary ones.

I was struggling to stop the spiral of thinking, the *ressassement*. It was chilly outside, but I couldn't find my red sweater and didn't want to waste time looking; it was suddenly deeply important to not waste a moment. I ran downstairs for one of the waxed coats behind the second kitchen door.

I found the light switch, flicked it on, a single halo of fluorescent tubing illuminated the stove. Sediment beneath my feet, dirt Graves had tracked in the last time.

I ran outside in my dirty bare feet. It was dark but I could see the wet grass catching the moonlight. My feet were soaked by the time I made it to the shed. I had left it unlocked. A fleeting worry that I would find the mythic intruder I'd once imagined living there. Did Lucy's father have his own mythic intruder, is that why he had installed the surveillance system?

I noticed one of the desk drawers slightly open. There was a screwdriver inside, old cigarette butts in a shot glass, assorted pens, broken white erasers. Ink had spilled along the bottom, staining the wood. Like the fabric grain of my bloodied dress as a child. It smelled a little. I slammed it shut. Ash-dust. I switched on the projector and pulled down the screen, tying the string in the metal loop. It snapped as

I knotted it and the screen flew back up, webs shuddered all around.

I was so physically and emotionally exhausted that I could barely reason with myself to figure out how to fix it. In a panic, I looked for my phone and realized I had left it in the house. There was a moan from somewhere in the woods, an unhinged animal. A spider caught the light and moved across the floor in tandem with the sound.

Graves had left a notebook open by the cracked back window and the pages flapped in the draft. I went to examine the contents of the second drawer and found a French souvenir lighter and some candlesticks, unsmoked cigarettes and more pens. Inside the next one, a candle snuffer on a long metal rod and some sage twigs in bundles. An ancient tourist pamphlet for the town named on the lighter. Three dead spiders on their backs, legs like retracted claws. A camping knife and more notebooks, filled with strange writing. The blade had a thick plastic handle and a leather sheath. There was a digital clock on the desk. Hacked bars of red and grey saying 3:00. Too neat to be real. I pushed it over and listened to it crash on the concrete floor. Dust again, even in the dark. There was a colorful Mexican blanket folded under the window. I went to get it and brought it with me to the orange rug, laid down, zipped my jacket and placed the blanket over my knees.

When I woke up, Graves was standing over me.

"Hi."

"What are you doing here?"

"It's our usual meet time."

"You didn't answer my calls."

"Sorry, I was busy. I'm allowed some time to myself," he said.

"You are."

"What are *you* doing here?"

"Couldn't sleep last night."

"I want to tell you something."

"Yes?"

"Why don't you get dressed or whatever."

"We usually get undressed."

"Not today."

"Okay." I pushed the blanket to my ankles and lifted my knees. He wouldn't look directly at me.

"Get up."

"Why?"

"I can't talk to you when you're like this."

I stood up and wrapped the blanket around as a skirt, tucking one edge into the waist like men do with towels. With my right hand I pulled my hair back into a ponytail, secured with a rubber band from the opposite wrist. He moved away when I tried to touch him. "What's wrong?"

"Nothing." The calm eyes swept the room.

"What did you want to tell me?"

"I'm leaving."

"What?"

"I have to go away for a little while."

"Where?" He wouldn't answer.

"I'll be back, and we can resume."

"Resume our relationship?"

"I'm not sure we have one."

"So tell me what you mean."

"You and your ultimatums."

"There's no ultimatum—"

"I told you. I haven't made up my mind about anything."

"What?"

"Whatever."

I said, "What if I wasn't around. How would that make you feel?"

"What do you mean?"

"Like, what if I wasn't here?"

"Like, science fiction?"

"What is wrong with you?"

"I have to go," he said. I stared at him, waiting for the punchline, for him to tell me it was a joke. Another test. He just looked at me, calm as ever, then turned and left without closing the door.

XXXVIII

I had managed to wash my hair and put on the red sweater (it had been in the bedroom all along), the gold necklace and a pair of jeans for Lucy's arrival. The plan had been to vacuum and prepare drinks in the living room, but I'd been unable to get out of bed for days. Graves wouldn't answer my calls. And with each call I felt more ashamed. All I could think of was how it had felt at the beginning, and how it had lasted until it didn't.

I had fascinated him enough to sustain our connection for two months. He had to do very little—arrive and pick me up, and put me down when he wanted to leave. I must have done something to make him retract. This became my focus, the thing to solve, superseding the cut on my back. That masochistic toil, to go back over every day. If I could find a pattern to it, I could solve his disappearance. Science.

The bell chimed, wet as ever, and I went to the front door, slowing opening it inward. Lucy stood there smiling, holding a bouquet of daisies. She hugged me tightly and I held onto her, pushing my fingers into her back through her jacket. Drawing away she held me at arm's length and asked, "What happened to you?"

"I need your help with something."

"Anything."

"Remember you mentioned how there are video cameras placed all over the house, some kind of insane surveillance."

"Your Josephine texted me once, asking if there was anything like that."

"What did you tell her?"

"I gave her the login and password for the setup."

"Lucy."

"I'm kidding."

"Oh, okay, but does something like that exist?"

"Yeah. I never looked at it, but the police used it when they thought someone had gone into the shed."

"Can you give it to me?"

"It's written on the paper on the fridge."

"Are you hungry?" I asked.

"I'm okay, but there is one thing I want to do right away."

"Oh, really?"

"Will you come with me to the cemetery? It's the anniversary of my grandfather's death," Lucy said.

"I didn't realize he was buried there."

"Yeah, that was his favorite place to be. The original house was torn down when my parents built this one. I'm sorry the daisies aren't for you."

I laughed. "Can you give me a half an hour?" I asked.

"For sure, I kind of want to take a nap."

"Which room do you want?"

"I'll stay in the green one, that's where I slept when I was little."

"I haven't even gone in there yet."

"It's sweet, you should come see."

"I'll be up in a little."

"Come get me when you're ready."

XXXIX

Lucy and I walked to the cemetery. The walk took an hour, and she comforted me all the way. The video footage was clear enough. There I was, naked on the rug. And he went to the drawer and came back to me. Three neat, clinical movements and he put everything away, then returned to push inside me again and carry on. It had been grainy and dark, lit up in green like a paranormal video on an old show about hauntings, but quite real enough.

After we dropped the daisies and made our way back, I told Lucy I had to do some work in the shed. She seemed pleased. Told me stories about playing on the floor, watching movies on the wall. I wanted to clean it before she went back in, so it would be the same as when she was a child. I rolled film and stacked boxes. Dragged a broom across the floor. When it was all tidy, I switched off the lights. Pulled the steel handle behind me and yelled. I looked down. My finger was caught in the door.